harmony for christmas

DANSBORO CROSSING SERIES

AVERY SAMSON

Editor: My Brother's Editor

Cover Designer: Rachel Webb

Cover Photo: kelpfish/depositphotos.com

contents

one

HARMONY

WHO KNEW the world could be so loud? Don't get me wrong, I'm grateful for everything I've been given. Sometimes, though, I wish I could just disappear for a while.

No one told me when I climbed on that stupid picnic table and belted out Kelly Clarkson that my life would become one whirlwind after another. Now people belt out Harmony Ellis at the top of their lungs, which is weird since that's me.

Tonight is just like every other night when I'm on tour. Greeting fans and singing has become my life. I've just walked off stage, hot and sweaty, to find fans lined up and down the hallway to my dressing room.

Of course, I greet them as I walk by. Without them, I'd be sunk. But, just once, I'd love to walk right out the back door, shower, and flop into bed with a good book. I can't even hide at my parents' house tonight because the one time the tour comes to Austin, they're on vacation somewhere else.

"Harmony. Hurry, sugar, we need to get you changed so you can meet your fans," Robin, my assistant, says.

It will be clothing change number five for me tonight. As quickly as possible, I change, and someone touches up my hair and makeup. Wasn't there a time when musicians simply flopped in their dressing rooms all sweaty after a concert while fans drank, smoked and shot the bull? Whatever happened to that?

"How many are there tonight?" I ask.

"Not that many," she answers. She opens the door and security starts sending them in. It's the same thing everywhere. They fangirl, I gush humbly, they take selfies, we take PR photos, they're finally escorted out, and I prepare for the next group. I love them, but I'm mentally exhausted.

"There's my rowdy girl." I turn around at the sound of a familiar voice.

"Travis?" I can't believe my eyes. Standing in front of me is a man I graduated from Dansboro Crossing high school with. It seems like a hundred years ago. "I can't believe it's you."

"In the flesh." Travis Rayburn was always the guy everyone wanted to hang out with. He wasn't necessarily one of the cool kids, but he was always fun. If Travis was around, you were guaranteed to have a good time.

"Well, are you just going to stand there gawking, or are you going to give me a hug?" He doesn't have to ask twice. I throw myself at him, and he spins me around with my feet off the floor.

"I can't believe you're here," I say when he sets me back on my feet. "How long has it been?"

"Five or six years at least? Since graduation anyway. How do I look?" He sucks in an almost non-existent gut and flexes his arms.

"Better than any man should." I'm not kidding, he does look good.

"Well, you look like a million bucks."

"Hey, do you have time to hang out?" I ask. "I don't have that many more people to greet, then we could get something to eat. I'm dying for some real Tex-Mex."

"Sounds perfect," he agrees.

I motion to Robin who shows Travis to a chair in the corner. He settles in, and I go back to work. Half an hour later, I'm ready to go.

"Where are you taking me?" I ask Travis as we climb into his car.

Robin was not happy when I told her we were going to get dinner, just the two of us. She argued about taking security until I finally put my foot down. Travis isn't a small man, and he can handle anything that may arise. Besides, he'll know some backwoods place to eat around here where no one will bother us.

"Do you mind a drive? I was thinking about getting out of town. There's a little place that serves the best chili rellenos you'll ever put in your mouth."

"That sounds amazing. The farther, the better." He gives me a strange look but doesn't say a word. We drive in silence for a few minutes before I can't stand it anymore. "Have you heard anything from the rest of our classmates?"

"You heard Brontë had a baby and married some rich guy?"

"I did. I can't believe she moved back. It seemed like she was the one who was the most likely to get out of that town." We run through the rest of the class.

It seems that Travis is the guy who keeps up with everyone. After I left for Nashville, I drifted away from my friends. I just didn't have time to keep in touch.

We pull up outside of a tiny restaurant with only a small sign advertising that they're open. I hop out of the car and meet Travis by the door. He pulls it open to a mix of spices that makes me sneeze. We find our seats and pull out the menus from behind the napkin holder. Following Travis's lead, I order the rellenos.

"Tell me everything you've been doing in the last couple of years. Don't leave out anything, I want to hear it all," I say placing my chin in my hand.

"I made it into law school."

"Oh my gosh. Really? You always were smart."

"Thanks." He blushes. "That's about it. I've been eyeballs deep in school forever now. Besides, you have the exciting life. Tell me everything about it."

"It's a lot, I can tell you that."

"Do you not enjoy it?" he asks.

"Do I enjoy it? That's a very good question, counselor. Some days." I shrug.

"Not a counselor yet. I still have to pass the bar. What's going on with you, though?" Damn, he's not going to let me steer the conversation to something safer.

"I think I'm just getting burned out. We have a break for the holidays that I was hoping to spend with Mom and Dad, but they're on a cruise. The idea of going back to Nashville for Christmas just doesn't appeal to me right now. I think if I could just get away for a while without anyone around, I could reset."

"Like a silent retreat," he says.

"Exactly. Only I don't want to go to some spa and be pampered. I don't know if I really know what I want."

The server appears with our dinner. Travis wasn't lying. The first bite of relleno melts in my mouth, then it lights it on fire. It's the perfect combination. I power through my meal like I haven't eaten in weeks.

When I'm done, the server replaces my plate with one containing flan. I haven't had flan in years. Come to think of it, I can't remember the last time I dared to eat dessert. Not all of us can be Reba thin naturally.

"What would happen if I had the perfect place for you to unwind?" Travis asks as I'm debating licking the plate clean. "Basic living, quiet, no one flitting around you."

"I'd be alone for Christmas?"

"Not exactly, but it would be as close as you can get. I'll be there."

"I don't know," I say, scrunching my eyebrows at him. "This isn't some weird sex thing, is it?" Travis laughs. Okay, so he's obviously no more into me now than he was in high school. "Okay, okay, you don't have to act like I was suggesting we adopt five kids together."

"I think my boyfriend would have something to say about that," he says. Oh. Ooooh! He grins at me as it sinks in.

"How did I not know this in school? Is he going to join us for Christmas?"

"Maybe. Anyway, I think you should come home with me. When was the last time you ate chicken fried steak at The Hungry Heifer? Or attended the Christmas parade on a horse lit with lights?"

"You have a valid point. I do love a good lit horse." I seriously debate his crazy idea. Do I really want to go home with a man I haven't seen in years? Yeah, I kind of do. "Okay, I say we throw caution to the wind and do it."

"That's how you got famous in the first place."

"I'll try not to let you video me singing on a park bench this time," I quip. "Unless the mood strikes me. Ooh, I could do Kelly Clarkson sings Christmas stuff. That might get me noticed." I wink at him. He sort of is the reason I got a recording contract. My performance was all over the internet the next day. "You should represent me someday."

"I'm not really planning on contract law."

"Yeah, but you know us celebrities, we get into all sorts of mischief."

"Then you'll be the first to get my business card. If I pass the bar."

"Pfft," I snort with a wave of my hand. "Piece of cake."

We leave the restaurant and drive back to the hotel. Travis sits on the couch in the living room of my suite while I pack some of my stuff. I'll let Robin get the rest of it later. I don't see any reason to take everything for a short stay.

He helps me haul my suitcase down to his car. I debate calling Robin to let her know what I'm doing, but opt for a text instead. After I send it, I turn off my phone so she can't start an argument about staying here.

"An hour and a half, I'll have you at your new accommodations, my lady," he teases.

"I can't wait." I drift off for most of the drive. Did I mention how totally exhausted I am? Even visiting with Travis can't keep me awake. He rousts me when we pull up in front of a small home in the middle of nowhere. I forgot he grew up on a ranch outside of our hometown.

"We need to be quiet," he warns as we park. "I'll get your bag." He unlocks the door and leads me to a tidy bedroom. He's right, there are no bells and whistles here. I'm too tired to care, though.

He shows me the bathroom in silence and then whispers that he'll be on the couch. I feel bad about kicking him out of the bedroom for about two seconds after my head hits the pillow.

* * *

The next morning I'm woken by noise coming from one of the other rooms. I lay staring at the ceiling for a full minute trying to remember where the heck I am.

Then it hits me, I came here with Travis last night. He promised me a restful Christmas. and without a second thought, I blindly went with him like a lemming. Sitting up, I throw my feet over the edge of the bed and touch the cold floor.

With the fuzziest pair of socks I have on, I slowly open the bedroom door. Someone is in the kitchen moving around. Has to be Travis. No matter what, I appreciate everything he's trying to do for me. I need to thank him for the effort before explaining I'll be fine flying back to Nashville for the holidays. The last thing I want to do is butt in on somebody else's Christmas.

Quietly, I pad down the hallway to the kitchen. Sure enough, he's standing at the stove with his back to me making breakfast. How he's surviving the cold house in nothing but a pair of jeans I don't know. I slide up behind him and throw my arms around his waist.

"Thank you so much for this," I begin, hugging him tightly. "You really are one of the best. I can't believe you went out of your way to help me."

It strikes me that he is as rigid as a board. Yesterday when Travis hugged me, I don't remember him being this lean. Nor do I remember him being so uptight. I don't think this is Travis. But if it's not Travis, who in the hell is it?

"Oh my gosh, you're not Travis," I gush turning loose of the stranger. The man turns as I back up across the room. I'm about to run when I realize that he looks very similar to my friend.

"Beau?" How could I forget that Travis has a brother? "I'm so sorry. I thought you were Travis." His eyebrow raises. "I don't normally go around grabbing strange men. Well, I guess you're not really strange, but you're certainly not Travis." He continues to stare at me.

"Anyway, do you know where Travis is? He said yesterday that I should come join him for Christmas, but I thought that meant he would be here. Not you. Not that you can't be here. I mean it's your home. Isn't it? I'll just grab my bag and skedaddle right on back to Austin. My assistant will feel better about that anyway. She likes me close where she can keep an eye on me." He's still staring at me.

"Oh my gosh, who is this?" I ask when a big yellow dog rises from a dog bed I missed in the corner. He wags his tail as he approaches me. There's one thing I can't hide. I love dogs. Dropping to my knees, I pull him into a hug. "Who's the best boy?" He licks my face, and I hug him one last time before standing again.

"Okay, well it was nice seeing you. Tell Travis I'll catch a ride back with someone. I just have to think of someone willing to give me a ride back. No matter, it's not your problem. So, yeah, take care."

I don't know what to do, so I just stand frozen while both Beau and the dog watch me. Who am I kidding, no one can take me back to Austin but Travis. Hopefully, he's still asleep somewhere in this small house. Finally, my gaze lands on the man standing across from me.

"Eggs?" he says holding the skillet up. I debate my options for a moment.

"Yes, thank you. I'm starving. I think the fresh air is making me hungrier than normal." He slides the fried eggs onto a plate and sets it on the table. "I can't remember the last time I had fried eggs." He adds a couple of pieces of bacon to my plate. "Bacon too. Wow." Jesus, why do I just keep talking?

"What's your dog's name?" Yep, still talking.

"Reacher."

"Ahh, yes, okay." I rack my brain for something else, but nothing comes. I really hope my friend shows up soon. "About Travis—"

He slides a note across the table to me. It explains that Travis had to return to Austin late last night for some sort of emergency meeting this morning. He says he'll be back later today and to not let Beau intimidate me. Easy for him to say. Has he met his mute brother?

"Well, at least he'll be back later today," I say between bites.

"Doubt it."

"Why? What's happened? He promised he would be here too. Did someone get hurt, because that would be horrible—" Panic begins to rise inside me as I babble on.

"Snowed in," he says cutting me off. I jump up and rush to the window. Sure enough, the landscape is covered in more snow than I remember ever seeing growing up. This part of Texas rarely gets snow, so when it does, everything comes to a screeching stop.

"Shit," I moan. "Now what do I do?" I turn to look at Beau, but he just shrugs. Great. Stuck in a cabin with a grunting Neanderthal. Christmas doesn't get much worse than this.

two

BEAU

SO. Many. Words. I don't think I've heard someone talk so much in this house since...ever.

Had I known Travis had a guest in tow last night when he showed up, I would have at least put on a shirt this morning. I might have even made more of an effort at breakfast. But when I heard him slip back out early this morning, I figured that was that. I know his schedule keeps him busy. I don't think twice about him coming and going now.

"So there's this whole thought that by cutting out the bad carbs from your diet—" I tune her out again. It didn't go unnoticed that she tucked into her breakfast like she hadn't been fed in years. A few carbs might do her good.

She's staring at my last piece of bacon though she's still rambling on about diets and calorie counts. She looks like she's considering starting an affair with breakfast meat.

"Here," I growl holding my bacon out to her. Reacher sits up in his bed hoping I'm talking to him.

"Oh no. You should eat that. I've had more than enough to last me for the day," she chirps. Is that what they call it when everything she says sounds like it's an audition for a movie about cute woodland creatures?

"Take it," I try again. This time, she carefully reaches for the bacon. She takes a tentative bite as I watch how her pouty lips close around it. Jesus, I need to get laid more. The last thing I need is to fantasize about Travis's houseguest.

"Oh my gosh," she exclaims suddenly. "I haven't even introduced myself. How much ruder can I be? First, I grope you in your kitchen thinking you're Travis, not that I'm the type of woman who just randomly gropes any man. Anyway, I'm Harmony Ellis." She extends her hand to me.

"I know who you are." Why does my hand tingle when I take hers in mine? Does she feel it? She must because she jerks her hand back to her side of the table. Or maybe she just finds me repulsive. I'm not too concerned either way.

"You do?" Her soft blue eyes grow wide.

"Mmm," I grumble getting up from the table. There's no way I'm telling her that I have her first album nestled among my mother's vinyl collection. I've preordered the second one for the moment it's released. It wasn't just a fluke that she landed a recording contract once that video went viral. She's got talent.

Turning on the hot water at the tap, I ignore her while I wash up the dishes. Mom always insisted she didn't want a dishwasher, and I've never gotten around to installing one. With just me living here, it's not that hard to hand wash the dishes. Of course, the chatterbox notices.

"You don't have a dishwasher?" She steps next to me as she places her plate in the sink. Her warm arm brushes mine. Thoughts of licking every inch of that skin flood my brain. I'm going to have to get out of here for a little while if

I want to save my sanity. "Do you mind if I take a quick shower?"

"Mmm," I grunt again. She almost knocks me out with her brilliant smile before she walks toward the bathroom. Is that humming I hear? When the bathroom door closes, I hurry to pull on the rest of my clothes. "Come on, boy." Reacher springs to his feet and follows me out of the kitchen.

I step into my insulated coveralls and boots by the back door of the mudroom and walk outside. The snow reaches halfway up my calf. For an area that rarely has snow, that's crazy.

Last time it snowed like this I was a kid. Travis and I spent the day sledding down an old dirt water tank that's behind the house. School was canceled for days, and except for checking hay, my parents stayed snuggled up on the couch watching old movies.

There's not much I can do out here in this weather. The horses need to be fed, but not until this evening. I was smart enough to put hay out for the cattle yesterday. They'll be good for a few days without feed. I need to keep an eye on their water, though. If it freezes too hard, they won't be able to break up the ice.

I guess that leaves carrying more firewood from the barn to the mudroom. I whistle for Reacher who's bounding through the snow checking all his favorite spots. He runs to my side panting and watches as I load my arms with logs.

"What can I do to help?" Harmony asks the moment I step inside the mudroom. Her hair is still wrapped in a towel from her shower, but she has on a pair of rhinestone covered jeans, a fuzzy red sweater, and thick socks. "Do you want me to put a couple of logs on the fire?"

"Sure," I say handing her two pieces of firewood. That should keep her busy while I go for the next load. When I return, she's organized the firewood that was already there into a neat stack at one end of the wall.

She's also wiped all the snow off Reacher. He stands at the kitchen door wagging his tail. Chances are good he's already found his new best friend. Traitor.

"I thought that the wood that's already warm, we could use first," she says. Makes sense. "Where can I find kindling? We're running a little short."

The next time I enter the house, I bring another stack of wood and a bucket of kindling. "Oh, perfect." She takes the bucket from my hands. "It's nice and toasty in there now." I have visions of an inferno shooting out the top of the chimney.

"That should do it," I announce on my last trip. My back is starting to complain, and there's only so much firewood that can fit against the wall.

"Good. I have the kettle on for hot chocolate." She seems more excited about the drink than I would think possible. "I even found some marshmallows." She watches me set the last of the wood down, then leads me into the main part of the house.

"I thought I might make a coffee cake for this afternoon if that's okay with you." She looks over her shoulder at me. "Is that all right?"

She stops and turns to look at me. I just now realize that I've stopped somewhere between the kitchen and mudroom to stare at her. Who is this woman who makes hot chocolate and coffee cake on a whim?

It takes everything I have to even my face back out from the scowl that graces it. I would make a snide comment except she looks worried. She can't possibly think that I wouldn't be okay with a piece of warm, brown sugar-covered goodness. Would she?

"I'm sorry," she says, her shoulders slumping. "My sister always tells me I can be too much."

"Your sister is a bitch." Good Jesus, did I just say that out loud? I watch as Harmony bites on her bottom lip as she studies me. Would it be too much if I offered to bite that lip with *my* teeth? Then she laughs.

"So you know my sister then."

"Not really. I remember Travis complaining about her." Harmony's sister had a reputation for being the Regina George of Dansboro High School according to Travis. I didn't know her personally, which I'm not sorry for. "I shouldn't have said that."

"Oh my gosh, Beau Rayburn has almost said a full paragraph that doesn't contain any grunting," she teases. I roll my eyes and walk past her into the living room. "I bet you're exhausted from the exertion. Have a seat, and I'll get our drinks."

She flits into the kitchen as the kettle starts to scream. "I'm surprised you even have hot chocolate, especially the good stuff. I pegged you for a black coffee only kind of guy."

I shrug as she sets the mug in front of me on the coffee table. Nothing is more boring than drinking the same thing every day. It's why I learned how to cook. I don't get into town very often, and I can't eat the same old thing day after day.

Studying my drink, I see she's not just added marshmallows, but nutmeg on top. She's even found a candy cane to stick in it. It takes me a moment to figure out how to drink the stupid stuff.

"Do you just make girly drinks?" I mumble to myself.

"Oh, you think that's a girly drink. Just wait." Well, I

thought I said it to myself. The woman must have ears like a bat. I'll have to remember that next time. "So what do you do around here for fun when you're snowed in?"

"We don't get snowed in."

"Yeah, but how about on your days off? What do you do for fun? Got any board games?"

"They take more than one player, so no." I feel my scowl returning as she looks around the room.

"You might be the only man I know with a television but no video game console." There is no way I'm telling her that I either read or sketch in my downtime.

I was always good at drawing, and I'm even better now. There are a couple of my works in one of the small galleries in Austin. The sales from them help supplement my retirement fund. I even won the art fair my senior year of high school, but she's too young to remember that.

"Travis said you don't have satellite internet," she says. Travis has a big mouth. "How do you check emails or Google anything?" I shrug again.

To be honest, I don't miss it that much. There is a point on top of the hill behind the house where I can hit the cell phone tower. I'm usually up there every other day or so. It would probably give her a heart attack to know that I don't have social media of any kind. If I need to, I can always go to the library in town.

"Hey, I have an idea. Do you get TV reception out here?"

"Should." I have a tower on the side of the house that picks up a couple of the local channels out of Austin. I do watch the weather forecast from time to time.

"When was the last time you got hooked on a daytime soap?"

"Never."

"You are in for a treat then." She grabs the remote and a

blanket and moves to the couch next to me. Pressing the remote, she hunts through the five channels until she lands on something that meets her approval.

"Oh, this is a good one. So, that guy's Andre. He's the head of a large network of spies." She continues to lay out the entire plot of the show for me. I'm not really paying attention, but I like when she throws the blanket over us and settles next to me.

Damn if she's not right. Half an hour later I'm completely obsessed with this shit. This is dangerous. I can just imagine the ranch falling apart around me while I'm engrossed in my "stories."

Tossing back the blanket, I stand. I grab the empty mugs and walk into the kitchen to put them in the sink. It's getting close to lunchtime anyway. Usually, I just grab a quick sandwich before heading back out to work. I wonder if she likes sandwiches.

"What are we having?" She's followed me into the kitchen.

"Grilled ham and cheese?" I don't know why I'm asking. I guess she can either eat what I make or go hungry. It's not like I'm running a bed and breakfast here.

"Yum. With soup?"

"Sure," I agree.

"I'll do the soup while you do the sandwiches." I'll show you something I want to do, I almost say. Instead, I just grunt in agreement.

Throwing myself into making sandwiches helps reroute my mind back to what's important instead of on my sexy new housemate. At least until she sidles up to me at the stove. She's humming again as she pours the can of soup into a pan.

"You're humming," I point out.

"Am I?" She adds milk to the tomato soup and begins to stir it. "I guess I am. Ever get something stuck in your head that you can't quite get right? I've had a song dancing around up there since I got here. I keep thinking that it'll either leave or turn into something."

I study her as she stirs the soup. "I know, you think I'm crazy." I'm sure I have a scowl on my face that leads her to believe that.

"I don't think you're crazy," I answer. "Not for that anyway."

"Oh my gosh." She hip-bumps me. "Did you just make a joke? Who are you, and what did you do with grumpy Beau?"

"I'm not grumpy," I mumble. She grins up at me. "Whatever."

"You're about to burn the sandwiches," she adds.

"Shit." I quickly turn off the burner and slide the sandwiches onto a plate. By the time I set them on the table, Harmony has bowls full of soup to add.

We each take our place across from each other. Reacher ignores my command to move to his pillow and plops down next to her. She takes a bite and moans. I have to hide a smile knowing she likes something I've made.

"Now that's a good sandwich," she exclaims. I watch as she chews and swallows. It's the first time I ever remember thinking eating is sexy, but she makes it look like food porn. "You know, I don't think there is anything better than a grilled cheese and tomato soup on a wintery day. It just makes you feel warm all over. Those ads weren't lying."

I like this meal as well as the next guy, but I'm not sure that I'd call it the best for a wintery day. Mom made a mean beef and vegetable stew that was right up there at the top.

But if I had to say what was the best, then it would be none other than—

"Chili."

"You're cold?"

"No," I sigh. "Chili is best on a winter day."

"I don't know. I've never had your chili. Can't make a ruling until then." I know she's teasing me with her flippant answer, but she's just waved the red flag in front of my face.

"We'll have it tomorrow," I growl.

"So not kicking me out yet I see," she says. Her smile is both sly and glorious. Damn, this girl is getting under my skin. I don't know if I can handle her for long. I guess that all depends on Mother Nature.

"Not yet anyway."

three

HARMONY

I JUST WANT to point out that for all of Beau's grumbling, his butt is firmly planted on the couch in front of the television when the next soap opera comes on.

Naturally, he pretends to ignore me when I explain the show's premise, but his mumbled "ridiculous" doesn't escape me. When a talk show starts, he firmly turns the TV off plunging us into silence again.

"I have a question," I say when he stands to poke at the fire.

"Not surprised," he mumbles under his breath.

"I heard that." I give him my best scowl. "Any who, when do you decorate for Christmas?" There is absolutely nothing indicating that my favorite holiday is quickly approaching. No lights, no tree, no stockings over the mantle, not even the promise of cookies to be decorated. "Are you one of those psychos who wait until Christmas Eve to put everything up?"

"Are you one of those psychos who leave decorations up year round?"

"No, not yet. I have a strict rule that everything goes up the day after Thanksgiving and comes down the day after the New Year," I inform him. "I'm not that crazy. Yet." I grin at him, but he stares back like he's harboring a serial killer. Finally, he turns and tosses another log on the fire.

"I don't decorate," he says with his back to me.

"I'm sorry, what?" Now who's the serial killer? "Excuse me, I thought I heard you mumble something about not decorating. I must need my hearing checked." I tug on my ear for emphasis.

He watches me as I stand and take an elaborate turn around the room. "Hmmm...it's too late for a menorah. Are you a Kwanza person?" I have several friends back in Nashville who celebrate Hanukkah and Kwanza. I've participated in both.

"No." The corner of his mouth lifts slightly. His eyes still track me as I return to the couch.

Why do I like that so much? Usually, a guy watching me that intently just gives me the creeps, and being somewhat famous means that happens a lot. But I find I don't mind it so much when it's Beau.

"I used to, when Travis was home. No reason to for just me."

"I assumed Travis came home every year for Christmas."

"Not always." I wait for him to elaborate, but he doesn't. I'm not surprised anymore by his silence. I've resigned myself to pulling every single word out of him.

"Well, he's coming this year so we should decorate. Besides, I bet Reacher would like a tree. Wouldn't you?" I say ruffling the dog's ears. He hasn't left my side since we sat down. I think it's starting to irritate Beau. Too bad. I'm not giving up the only friendly thing in this house. "So, where do you keep your tree?"

"Outside. In the ground. Where they belong."

"Oh." Maybe I can make some garland to hang at the very least. "Okay. I'll think on that later. I did promise coffee cake with our afternoon tea. You have tea, don't you?"

He stomps into the kitchen, opens a cabinet, and pulls out a box. Setting it on the counter, he turns to glare at me. "Fine. Now shoo so I can make the cake. Go on. Go sit in a chair and keep me company." I make go-away swooshes with my hands.

Beau looks at me with one eyebrow raised, but he moves to slump against the wall at the kitchen table. He leans half against the back of the chair and half against the wall. His long legs are stretched in front of him, and his elbows rest on the table and chair back.

How come when a woman sits like that, she's being "unladylike," but it's fine for a man? He looks casually alpha male. It's like business casual, but in sexy man speak.

"This is my great, great, grandma's recipe. Fortunately for you, I have it memorized." I tap my temple. "It has all the good stuff in it. Back then they didn't give a hot rat's ass about carbs."

"Hot rat's ass?" I catch a quick glimpse of white teeth before Beau manages to hide his smile. So, he can smile without a hole opening up and swallowing him whole. Miracles never cease.

"The same grandma who said you should never drink water, it'll rust your pipes."

"What did she drink instead?"

"Whiskey. What else."

"I think I like your great, great, grandma."

"Just wait until you try her coffee cake. She called it a which-what-who. I don't know why." I work at mixing the batter with a whisk I found in a drawer. When it's smooth, I pour it into a pan and add the brown sugar mixture on top. "Now, we just have to wait for it to bake. What can we do for thirty-five minutes?"

His gaze travels down my body and back up before his eyes meet mine. Was that a blush I saw creeping up from under the collar of his shirt? I must be imagining things. Too many soap operas, I'm sure.

"Do you have a deck of cards?" I ask.

"Should." He moves into the living room and digs around in a cabinet under a wall of bookshelves. Returning to the table, he dumps two decks in front of me. I've taken the chair across from where he was sitting.

"Do you know how to play go fish?"

"Or an adult game." He shuffles the cards and deals them out. "We'll start with gin rummy."

"Fine, but you know you want to secretly say 'go fish.'" I organize my cards. He shakes his head and cuts to see who goes first. I win the cut so I draw a card. Siding it into place, I toss a discard on the table. "Go fish."

He lets out a big sigh, Oscar-worthy really. Drawing a card, he studies his hand and then squints his eyes at me. Without looking away, he tosses down his discard.

"Fish," he mumbles. It makes me grin. Somewhere, way deep down, I believe Beau Rayburn has a sense of humor. The game continues back and forth until the buzzer on the stove vibrates.

"Hold that thought." Jumping out of my chair, I move to

the oven. The toothpick I use to check the coffee cake slides out clean proving it's ready. "Smells so good," I moan setting the pan on the counter. "Tea?"

"Sure." He watches as I move around the kitchen. He has a surprisingly large variety of tea selections. I chose an apple spice and set the kettle on one of the burners. Turning the knob, I wait for the click of the igniter, but nothing happens.

"You have to light it," he says leaning around me. "It's old." He pulls a match from a cute little jar behind the stove, strikes it, and lights the burner.

There's a moment when he's reaching for the match where his chest brushes against my back. I know it sounds crazy, but in that instance, my body heats to the point of boiling. It's almost erotic how good his touch feels.

He moves away in a blink, but my body still tingles everywhere he pressed against me. Lord, I'm losing it. I mean, it's been a long time since I've had time to press against a man, but this is ridiculous.

"I should cut...cake?" I mumble.

"Are you asking?" He moves back to his chair at the table. That tiniest of smiles appears again. Probably because his innocent touch has made me twitterpated. That's what my granny used to call it anyway. She said whenever my dad came to see my mom when she was in high school, she lost all her senses. But I'm not in high school, and we're not dating.

"No, I'm just letting you know I'm picking up a knife. In case you need to light any more burners suddenly." I sound more confident this time.

"Or you need to accost half-naked men cooking breakfast?"

"Mr. Rayburn," I say in mock offense. "I have never

accosted a man, half-naked or otherwise, in my life." His smile lasts a little longer this time. "Now, sir, eat your cake or else." I plunk a plate with a piece of the coffee cake on it in front of him.

"Or else what? You'll spank me?" My face flushes bright red. Quickly, I spin around to face the kettle praying that it whistles soon. He chuckles lightly behind me.

The word spank coming out of his mouth in a rough growl has an even stronger effect on my nether regions than the simple touch. Where's a good hand fan when you need one?

"Beau Rayburn! You are not the nice boy I always heard you were." I pour the mostly hot water over the tea bags and set the mugs on the table.

"I haven't been a boy in a long time." He manages to say it with a smirk before taking a slow bite of cake.

My sophisticated brain wants to push everything on the table to the floor, climb over it into his lap, and ride him like a five-cent horse in front of the drugstore. What my mouth does, however, is make a weird "eep" noise. He chuckles again.

"Did you just laugh?" I ask in fake astonishment. I even press my hand to my breastbone. "Did it hurt? Is the ground going to open up and swallow us?"

He rolls his eyes, and we eat in silence for a while. It's for the best. I don't think I can handle Beau's form of flirting if that was what he was doing.

"Were you flirting with me?" I ask on a whim. You won't know if you don't ask.

"No," he scowls. "That would be...exploitative of me."

"Jesus, do you read the dictionary in your spare time? Is that what you do for fun?" He looks at me with a raised eyebrow. "I'm just messing with you." I grin. "Would you like some more?"

"No, thank you," he says hesitantly. "I've got some chores I should be tending to outside."

"Oh, is that where you keep the Christmas decorations? Outside?" I can hope.

"You're not going to let this go are you?" He waits for me to answer, but I just stare at him until he rolls his eyes. "Yes, because stacked in boxes outside is the best place for Christmas decorations."

"They could be in the barn."

"They're not in the barn. Nothing but equipment and feed is in the barn. Probably the horses at this point."

"You have horses?" I ask a little more excited than I should be.

In my defense, what girl doesn't dream of owning a horse when she's growing up? I used to think about it all the time, but we lived in the middle of town, and my parents weren't about to take on the expense of owning a horse. No matter how many books about ponies I read, the answer was always no.

"I have two."

"Oh my gosh, two. You're horse rich."

"I don't think two makes me horse rich." The corner of his lips hitches up.

"Well, I have none. So compared to me, you're rolling in it. Can you ride them?"

"I can," he answers.

"Will you teach me sometime? There's a lot of things I want, but learning to ride is at the top of my reasonable wish list."

"Are there a lot of unreasonable things you wish for?"

"People seem to think so."

"Like?"

"Now, if I tell you all my secrets, how will I maintain my aura of mystery?"

"Pretty sure, you're a natural at that. Tell me one."

"One secret wish? Okay, but then you tell me one of yours." I wait until he nods. "I would really like to be able to wander outside of my home in just a T-shirt and sweatpants to water my plants without it making social media and then having to learn how my clothing choice makes me look."

"That one sounds reasonable."

"Well, apparently not everyone thinks so. Now it's your turn." I set my chin on my fist and give him my entire focus. I'll be amazed if he admits to anything personal. He just doesn't seem like that guy. I imagine he doesn't even admit to himself what he would like.

"I—" he starts before falling silent again. I don't move a muscle. He sighs and starts again. "I would like to date someone who doesn't want to sleep with me just for the bragging rights of bagging the town recluse."

Wow. I mean, wow. "Did someone actually do that?"

"Several." A faint flush creeps up his cheeks. "Never mind," he murmurs.

"Stay," I bark leaping to my feet. He freezes, and Reacher drops to his haunches. I dig around in the kitchen drawers until I finally find the one with all the junk that doesn't make sense anywhere else. Returning to the table, I slap a notepad and pen down in front of him. "I need their names. It's time they were taught some manners."

"You're going to defend my honor?" His face flushes a little redder, but his smile brightens.

"Damn straight. I've had a few of those too. Guys who just want to tell their friends that they bagged the newest

Nashville star. Not that I see myself as a star," I'm quick to add. "That's what the social media folks say."

His smile turns sweet as he stares back at me. Sweet and sexy, a lethal combination. "I guess I never thought of it happening to men. Makes sense, though. Well, you're safe with me. Not that I wouldn't sleep with you, just I wouldn't brag about it."

"Thanks?"

"Oh no, I mean, I'm sure it would be brag-worthy, I'm just classier than that. But, I'm positive it's very brag-a-licious to have sex with you. Oh, Lord." I cover my face with both hands. "Now I'm making up words to describe our sleeping together. I wish I could just stop talking."

I do finally stop the word vomit and peek through my hands at him. He's full-on grinning at me.

"Are you flirting with me?" he asks, throwing my words back from earlier.

"Could be. The jury's still out." He laughs, and my body heats at the deep rumble. "If so, how did I do?"

"It was different, but not bad."

I let my hands flop back to the table. Beau Rayburn has me completely intrigued. The same man who growled and snarled when he wasn't mute is also sweet and funny.

Why would any woman just want him for bragging rights? I mean, he's not too shabby in the looks department either. Okay, he's stupid hot in that lean cowboy kind of way, but I think there's also more than meets the eye. He has layers to him that beg to be explored.

"Did you just mumble that I have layers?" he asks.

"Did I say that out loud? Hmm, maybe?"

"Like Shrek?"

"You wish. No man can hold up to everyone's favorite ogre."

"Fair." Finally, he pushes out of his chair. "I really should get to those chores before it gets dark."

Before I can say another word, he's closing the door to the mudroom with Reacher in tow. Good, maybe I can get myself together before my next need to spew everything in my brain to the very man I find more intriguing than anyone I've met in a long time.

four

BEAU

I DON'T HAVE any chores that need to be done outside. I had to escape. It was either that, or I was in real danger of kissing her. She had me admitting to things that I've never told anyone, not even Travis. I'm positive he believes that all I want is an occasional lay, and they were great when I was younger. But, now I'm in my thirties, and I'd like something more.

I'm sure that Harmony sees me as rude, conceited, and overbearing. I, however, can see myself settling down with someone like her. No, not someone. Her.

Except, she's a rising star in Nashville, and I'm not leaving the family ranch, so there's no reason to start something. Now if I can just convince my body of that. Because, damn, it knows what it wants, and it's her.

"Hey, boys," I call to the horses stepping inside the barn. They're tucked inside one of the open stalls for warmth. I shake out some grain and toss another hay bale into the manger while Reacher tries to eat a frozen piece of manure.

"You wouldn't mind teaching a pretty girl how to ride would ya?" Neither of them answers. That's okay, I've gotten used to their stony silence. Seems we're alike in that way.

"Don't guess either of y'all know where to get a Christmas tree around here?" They ignore me.

Grabbing the axe out of the corner, I hike out through calf-deep snow in hunt of some sort of tree. Reacher chases through a couple of possibilities peeing on them in turn. I guess not those.

I'm not caving into her demand. It's just that she's trapped here, and I'm trying to be a good host. That's what I'm going to tell myself anyway. The fact I know her face will light up when I drag a Christmas tree inside has no bearing on it. Nope, no bearing at all. Just making a friend of my brother's comfortable.

"How about this one?" I ask the dog. "And if you lift your leg anywhere near, I'm chopping it off instead of the tree." He considers me for a second before moving on. I think it will be a suitable cedar tree. It's the only thing still green out here. Hopefully she's not allergic to them.

I chop it down and drag it through the snow back to the barn. With it propped up in the corner, I chop off some of the lower branches so it'll sit inside a bucket. It should fit inside my living room without taking up too much room. As the sun starts to set, I hoist the tree on my shoulder and walk to the house.

"Hey, I got you something," I announce when I open the front door. Some amazing aroma wafts through the air. My stomach rumbles in response. Reacher barks his approval.

"Is that a Christmas tree?" Harmony asks, rushing into

the room. Her look of excitement is the very one I was aiming for when I chopped this bad boy down. She does some kind of little happy dance in front of me while clapping her hands. How could anyone not want to spend all their time in this woman's orbit? Even if she does talk a lot.

"Here." I hold the bucket out until she snatches it from my hands. I motion to a spot near the front windows and lower the tree into it. "Needs water." She flits off into the kitchen and returns with the kettle full of tap water.

"I can't believe you brought me a tree. And it's a real one! It might be the nicest thing anybody's ever done for me," she gushes. Why would chopping down a tree make the top of the list? "After supper, you can help me make garland and paper snowflakes for it."

"What are we, in kindergarten?" When her face falls, I feel like an asshole. "I think I have some frozen cranberries we can defrost for the garland if you think they'll work."

She nods, but I can tell I've crushed her spirit again. I can fix this. "What is one thing you always wanted for Christmas but never got?" I follow her into the kitchen while she thinks.

"Other than a horse?" she asks.

"Other than a horse."

"I guess it would be one of those karaoke machines with all of the neon lights."

"Those are pretty cool. I always wanted a sled like you see people using in the movies. Mom used to watch Hall-mark movies starting in November. She kept telling me that a sled only works in the snowy states."

"You should go to one of the snowy states one Christmas. You could hire someone to watch the ranch." Her smile has returned, so I guess I'm forgiven.

"Maybe." She grows silent as she stirs something on the

stove. I don't like it. I know I complain when she talks nonstop, but it's better than silence. I fight the urge to find out if she's still mad at me.

I remember Mom complaining about Dad asking her that every time she wasn't her usual chipper self. Harmony isn't mine though. I don't get to worry about her happiness. Do I? It seems like I should have to earn that right.

"What are you making? It smells amazing."

"It's an old southern recipe that I think you're going to like." Her smile brightens a little more, and my heart skips a beat. I'm sure it's just from coming into the warmth from being outside. It couldn't possibly be because I'm falling for this girl after one day. "You have a weirdly well-stocked pantry," she adds.

"I visit Travis once a month and stock up."

"Good thing. I think it's snowing again." She motions toward the front windows. Turning around, I find soft flakes falling in the last of the sunlight. I've never seen it snow like this, especially in December. "I'm sorry you're trapped with me," she says.

"I'm not trapped."

"Ensnared?"

"Not that either."

"Ambuscaded?"

"Now who's been reading the dictionary?"

She throws back her head and laughs. When she spears me with her gaze again, her soft eyes dance with mirth.

Once again, I have to fight the urge to kiss her. It would be so easy to pull her into my arms and press my lips to her soft neck. But she has no means to escape me. I would be that letch taking advantage of her situation. I know my parents raised better sons than that.

"This needs to simmer for a while. How about we start

on the tree while we're waiting?" I would say the moment was broken by her change in conversation, but it's not. As a matter of fact, I don't know how I'll survive until the snow melts. Everything she says simply pulls me closer. "I have an idea. Do you have any construction paper?"

"Umm." I take a quick look around the kitchen. I haven't seen construction paper in years. "Maybe. It would be left over from when Travis was still in school. We can look in the office."

I lead the way through the mudroom into a small room where Dad kept his office. It's mine now, but I don't use it that often. The room is still filled with framed photos of us trapped in time before my parents passed.

"Your parents looked like movie stars," Harmony says softly. I lift my head from the desk drawer I'm searching through to see what she's looking at. It's a photo from their wedding.

"Yeah, everyone said they looked like a fairy tale."

"Is this you?" She's pointing to another photo of me in a Little League uniform next to Dad.

"It is. I think I was in first grade. Travis wasn't born yet."

"Then neither was I." She doesn't need to remind me that I'm ten years older than her. It feels like there is a lifetime between us. Sometimes Travis and I feel the same way.

"Y'all are so cute." She's studying one from a Christmas when I must have been twelve and Travis was two. I was always tall for my age, so cute is not the word I'd use to describe my awkward pre-teen self.

"Found some," I announce flopping an old pack of paper on the desk.

"I remember when your parents died. As an eight-year-old, I had no idea what to say to Travis. He was sad for so long." I grow still. I thought I did a good job at picking up the pieces for my little brother. It bothers me, even after all these years, to think of him mourning their loss. It was natural for him to miss them, but it still breaks my heart. "It was a car accident, wasn't it?"

"Yeah. They were coming back from Austin. They weren't sure if Dad tried to dodge a deer or fell asleep or what. The car rolled."

"I'm sorry," she says. Her gaze turns to me, her eyes shimmering with unshed tears. "I wish I had known what to say to Travis at the time. I truly am sorry."

"Mmm," I grunt. "It was a long time ago." Taking the construction paper, I return to the kitchen table. It still hurts to talk about their accident. It's easier just to forget. She follows me and adds some scissors and tape to the pile.

"I thought we could use the construction paper to make garland instead of popcorn and mushy cranberries."

"That's probably wise." I breathe a sigh of relief when she lets the subject of my parents' death go. There's so much more to her than people realize. I imagine just having her around when it happened helped Travis, even if she didn't know what to say.

She begins cutting the paper into strips while I tape the chains together. It's not long before we have a multicolored chain of garland.

"What are we doing for lights?" she asks.

I turn to study the tree. Even if I still had our Christmas lights, they wouldn't be working after all this time.

"I need to ride over to the neighbors and check on them tomorrow. I can see if they have any we can borrow. They're both older, so I need to make sure they're okay," I answer. "You can come if you don't mind riding one of the horses."

"Really?" She claps her hands with glee. "My first official horseback ride."

"You never rode a horse at summer camp growing up?"

"My parents couldn't afford summer camp, and none of my friends had horses. It's not like I could stay out here in high school to ride with Travis," she points out.

"No, I guess not. He never enjoyed it anyway."

"Yeah, so," Harmony says, pushing up from the table. "I say we hang this on the tree." She loops the garland around my neck several times before pulling me out of my chair.

"What about the lights?"

"It won't be that big of a deal to weave them in if we get some tomorrow. I just can't stand that naked tree even one more second." I follow her into the living room with a smile. "We'll work on making snowflakes for it next." Unwrapping the garland from around my neck, she begins threading it through the limbs.

"What do you need for snowflakes?"

"Copy paper, scissors, and paperclips."

"Okay." I return to the office for more supplies. Taking a moment to look around the room, I decide it's time to turn it back into a real office.

Maybe I should consider getting satellite internet so I can stay in touch with the world a little more. I could check my email more often than once every couple of weeks when I get around to it. The phone service would be reliable too. Not that I'm expecting a certain blond bombshell to keep in touch.

"Did you get lost?" that bombshell asks from the doorway.

"Mmm," I grunt as I walk past her carrying the supplies she asked for. Returning to my seat, I focus on cutting out snowflakes. Luckily, my art skills transfer to ornament making. Soon were both lost in the task. Harmony hums as she cuts on her creations.

"You're humming again," I say when I can't identify the tune.

"Sorry. It's driving me crazy. I can't quite catch it. Do you know what I mean?"

"I do." I understand exactly. My hands have been itching to draw her since I turned around this morning to see who had me in a death lock.

"My manager says to leave it alone, and it'll come out when it's ready." She shrugs her shoulders and studies my snowflakes. "You're weirdly good at this. How many do you have?"

"Ten or fifteen."

"That should be plenty. Should we hang them on our tree?"

Something about hearing the words "our tree" makes my heart warm. It's strange how much I'm starting to enjoy this Christmas. With just my brother and me, it's never been very festive. We just stopped trying years ago. There's only so much Yuletide cheer two single men are willing to do.

"What do you think?" she asks several minutes later when we have the snowflakes hung on the limbs.

"Not bad."

"Not bad?" she says with a puff. I check to make sure she's not upset, but she's smirking at me. "That's a work of art."

"Fucking Mona Lisa."

"That's better. Now how about some of my famous, but totally stolen recipe, shrimp gumbo?" She laughs.

"Can't. Too busy marveling at this masterpiece," I say, pointing at the tree.

"Smart-ass," she mumbles. Rolling her eyes, she shoves me toward the kitchen.

"Did you just cuss?"

"Yes, now get in the kitchen, asshat, before I change my mind and toss it all out the backdoor."

"I would hate all that good shrimp to go to waste. I'm sure this asshat will appreciate it more than the raccoons." She grins at me, and I follow her into the kitchen. At this point, I would follow her anywhere.

five

HARMONY

STAYING PERPETUALLY UPBEAT IS EXHAUSTING. I'm trying my best to make the best of an awkward situation. Being trapped in a house in the middle of nowhere with a man I don't really know was never at the top of my Christmas wish list.

It's hard because I can't get a read on this man. One minute he's growling at me, the next he's cracking a joke. It's enough to make my head spin.

Then there's the fact that every time he turns that simmering gaze on me it feels like he can see everything. I've never felt more exposed, and his eyes rarely drop below my face.

I can feel them on me now as I study his mom's old DVD collection. Do I bend over so I can see them better, thus waving my behind in his view, or do I continue to squint but stay ramrod straight? Oh, screw it.

"Hmm," he hums behind me when I bend over. What does that mean?

"Oh hey, you have one of my favorite Christmas rom-coms," I say before I can overanalyze the proportions of my ass and his response to said proportions. *While You Were Sleeping*.

I hold up the DVD when I turn around like it's a trophy. Who am I kidding? It is a trophy. I've had a girl crush on Sandra Bullock for years now, and in my humble opinion, this is one of her best.

"Whatever," he mumbles.

"Is that a yes whatever, please hook me up with a yummy movie featuring the all-time best man sandwich in history? Or whatever, as in I will literally cut my own eyes out if I have to watch a romance?" I mean, I can't read man grunt.

"It means whatever, as in whatever you want to watch," he answers. He smiles at me. I've noticed his smile is coming out a little more frequently now and, damn, if it doesn't make me melt a little bit every time. Stupid, sexy cowboy.

"I'll make a deal with you. We watch this first, then we can watch *Die Hard*, the other best Christmas movie ever. Wait, let me guess—"

"Whatever," we say in unison.

I shake my head and turn back to the ancient DVD player. With the movie in, I return to snuggle under the blanket on the couch. He clears his throat when I scooch next to him so he can share my blanket. The open credits begin, and I grab the bag of pretzels I found in his pantry.

"You agree *Die Hard* is a Christmas movie?" he asks quietly.

"If it has a Christmas tree in it, it's a Christmas movie," I answer. Out of the corner of my eye, I see him study me for a beat. Then with a barely perceptible nod, he turns back to the movie.

We watch the movie for the first half hour in silence. But I'd much rather talk to Beau.

"Can I ask you a question?"

"Mmm," he grunts. I'll take that as permission to continue.

"Why Reacher?" I stroke the dog's head. He hasn't really left my side all afternoon.

"What do you mean?"

"Why that name when there are a lot of good dog names out there? He looks like a Bruno or a Duke, so why name him Reacher?"

"He's big and blond. What else would I call him?"

"Okay, I get it now, I guess. What kind of dog is he?"

"I'd guess a mix of Great Dane and Lab. Travis dumped him here a couple of years ago. Claimed I was starting to talk to myself."

"I don't buy that," I tease. "You don't talk at all as far as I can tell, not even to yourself."

"I talk," he answers. From his tone, I would guess he's a little hurt by my observation. Truth hurts.

"You grunt and growl. You do not talk."

"So, I am Shrek then."

"There you go comparing yourself to the sexiest ogre in the history of cinema again." He tries to hide the smile that breaks across his face, but I see it plain as day. "What do you think, Reacher? Is he a closet conversationalist when no one is around?"

The dog barks in response.

"I didn't think so."

"Just watch the movie," he says with exasperation. He

can't fool me, there's still a hint of a smile on that handsome face. We sit in silence for another half hour.

"What are your thoughts on kissing?" I can't stand it. It's too easy to rile him up.

"What?" he says, sputtering.

"In movies. What are your thoughts on kissing in movies?"

"Jesus." He runs a hand through his short hair. "I don't know. It's fine, I guess." I let him settle back into the movie just long enough to drop his guard again.

"And sex?" I ask off-handedly.

"Harmony," he growls in warning.

"Am I flirting again?" I bat my eyelashes at him innocently. He scowls back with one eyebrow cocked.

"I don't know what you're doing, but you're driving me crazy."

"In a good way or a bad way?"

"I'm making some tea," he says, pushing off the couch. He turns to face me. "Would you like any?"

I have two ways I can answer this. Right now, I'm thinking I should probably look away from the bulge in his pants that hits me at eye level. Mouth level really. Would I like some of what he's hiding in those jeans? Yes, please. Do I want some tea? Whatever. Can I convince him to wrap a bow around that thing and call it my Christmas present?

"You're not helping," he growls again. My gaze drifts up to meet his stormy one.

"Yes?"

"How would you like it?"

"Excuse me?" He has to know what he's doing, right? I mean, this is too easy.

"Do you want it plain, with something in it, over ice? I

can probably find one of those old peppermint sticks if you want."

"However you want to give it to me is fine." I can actually feel my face heating.

Beau shakes his head as he walks into the kitchen. If I had said the same thing to Travis, it would have been an innocent conversation. Everything with Beau feels sexually charged. If the weather doesn't break soon, I should be able to melt the snow with my oversexed mind.

"I'm giving it to you hot and steamy," he says, setting a hot cup of tea on the coffee table several minutes later.

"Now I know you're flirting with me."

"Seems a little aggressive for flirting," he points out. "You should probably slap me into next week."

"Ooh, foreplay." An unexpected laugh bursts from Beau. It makes me laugh with him.

"You're a mess." He picks up another DVD and waves it at me. "*Die Hard*?"

"Yippee-ki-yay, Mother—"

"Harmony Ellis," he admonishes. "And here I thought you were a good girl." He winks, and if I was standing, my knees would have buckled. A wink, a smile, and a smart-ass remark? Who is this and what happened to the grouch I started with this morning?

"Define good."

He shakes his head again before popping the movie into the old player. I hear him mumble something under his breath, but I can't quite catch it.

"I'm sorry, what was that?" I ask. He stands back up to his full height and turns slowly to face me. His gaze is intense as it meets mine. My breath hitches at the severity.

"I said," he says just loud enough for me to have to lean toward him to hear. "You might need to be put over my knee." Before I can even process how fun that could be, he walks into the kitchen.

"Hey, you're going to miss the beginning," I yell. "And that's not all," I mumble under my breath this time. "Lord, Harmony. He might have just melted all of your girly parts into a puddle."

"Girly parts?" He's standing in the door of the kitchen holding a bag of chips. There's a knowing smile on his face.

"Like, uhh," I stammer, trying hard to come up with anything other than my nether regions I could have been referring to.

"I know what girly parts are," he answers, the smile turning into a shit-eating grin.

"I'm sure you do."

"Chips?" He offers me the bag, and I snatch it from his hands. Digging a massive fistful out, I cram them all in my mouth at the same time. Now maybe nothing stupid can come out of my mouth.

He's still watching me, but his face has morphed into something more like concern. I'm sure he's preparing to Heimlich chips from my windpipe at any moment.

"I brought you a beer too," he says.

"Mmm," is all I manage to get out.

Then, the worst thing I can think of begins to happen. It starts with a tickle in the back of my throat before progressing into my nose. I chew faster so I can swallow before the inevitable happens.

"Aaa-chooo."

I spray half-masticated chips all over the living room. My first thought is, how did I get all of those in my mouth? Then I'm faced with the fact that I just shot spit all over the coffee table of the one person I should be trying to impress so I don't get kicked out into the blizzard.

"Oh. My. Gosh," I say, turning to face him. "I'll clean that up. Reacher!"

The dog has sprung into action. He hoovers up the chips like he's finally found his mission in life. I dive to the ground to try and hold him back.

"Beau, help me."

He doesn't answer; he's too busy laughing. Not just a chuckle either. One of those deep in the belly, head thrown back, full body laughs. He's laughing so hard his eyes have started to water. Okay, it is sort of funny. Before I know it, I'm laughing just as hard. I turn loose of Reacher and collapse on the floor.

"Are you okay?" he asks around a burst of laughter. "You really are bad at flirting."

"Hey!" Yeah, I have to agree with him. One sexy spanking reference and I turn into a chip cannibal.

"You've sealed your fate as Reacher's favorite now," he adds. I place my hands over my already red face. How is it possible for it to grow even hotter? "Come on," he says, thumping the couch next to him. "Let's finish the movie."

I crawl over to the couch and slide onto the end. He teasingly moves the bag of chips to the other side of him. I shoot him a glare and punch him on the arm.

Before I realize it, we're sitting together with the blanket pulled over our legs. Reacher curls up next to me with his head on my leg. My life hasn't been this easy for a long time. That's how being with Beau feels. Easy.

We watch the movie in companionable silence until it ends. I'm in favor of moving to the next one, but Beau switches the input over to catch the news. The weather forecast is calling for even more snow as the temperatures continue to plummet. It even threatens of adding an ice storm on top of it. He'll be stuck with me forever at this point.

"I'm going to have to check hay and water tomorrow," he mutters.

"What can I do to help?"

"I'll have to take the tractor."

"I can help anyway. I promise I'm not totally useless."

"Who said you were useless?" he snarls. His scowl has me shrinking back against the couch. Reacher growls deep in his throat.

"I just—" I'm not sure what to say. Most of the time, I'm treated like the only thing I'm good for is dressing up and entertaining a crowd. My assistant even arranged for a caterer once when I had my family for Thanksgiving. I promise I can cook a turkey without assistance.

"We'll check on the neighbors in the morning," Beau says finally. His brow smooths back out which makes me relax again. "Then after lunch, we'll check around here." He nods and stands. "I'm heading to bed. I'll see you in the morning." With that, he turns on his heel and walks to the back bedroom.

"Okay, then, Reacher." I turn off the television and take the remains of our snacks to the kitchen. After checking the front door is locked, I turn around to find Beau standing behind me.

"I was coming back to do that."

"Oh. Sorry." We stand perfectly still, staring at each other. I'm not sure what I'm supposed to do next. I didn't realize I was breaking some sort of man rule by checking the door. Then he takes a step toward me. It's followed by another, and suddenly he's pressed against me.

His hand cups the back of my neck as his lips meet mine. They're warm and firm and, heaven help me, the best thing I've tasted ever. His tongue sweeps inside my mouth with a moan.

I'm not sure which of us made the noise, but I don't care. I just know I hope this never ends. I've never been kissed like I'm the very oxygen someone needs to survive, but that's exactly what it feels like.

It's over too soon sadly. Beau presses his forehead against mine as his chest heaves against me.

"Jesus," he mumbles. "I'm sorry." He stands straight and takes a step back.

I feel his gaze burn down my body and back up. He shakes his head. "Fuck." Before I can say, "yes, please," he's stomping back down the hallway.

"Wow," I whisper, touching my lips. Now how am I supposed to get to sleep knowing he's right down the hallway from me. "Come on, Reacher."

The dog happily follows me as I head to my bedroom. He might as well join me. Lord knows I'm not getting any sleep tonight.

six

BEAU

I CAN'T BELIEVE I kissed her. Wait. Yes I can. What I can't believe is that it took me so long to finally flip out and pin her against the wall to kiss her.

I fully expected her to throw open the door and take her chances freezing in the open countryside. Never did it cross my mind that she would kiss me back. And that's exactly what she did with her soft, warm lips. Thankfully, reason overtook me before it went any farther. I would like to claim that I can be a gentleman when put to the test.

But then, would a gentleman be leaning again the door-jamb to her room watching her curled up next to a giant dog in bed? I opened the door simply to insist Reacher go outside this morning. Something about her, though, holds me rooted in place. Maybe it's the golden hair splayed across the pillow, or the soft curves curled under the blanket, or the way she has her arm wrapped around my dog.

"You're starting to freak me out," she mumbles, pulling me from my fantasies.

"Sorry. Reacher, out."

The dog grunts, but he slides off the bed and out the door.

"You're spoiling him." Closing the door behind us, I roll my eyes at my reprimand. It takes me a few minutes to convince Reacher that he has to go outside to do his business.

I return to the kitchen to find her wrapped in the blanket from the bed and sitting in a kitchen chair. I should say something about last night. An apology is on the tip of my tongue when she speaks.

"Do you never get cold?"

"I guess." I look down at what I'm wearing. This time I have on a T-shirt instead of just jeans. My feet are bare though. I never think about it, being cold or hot.

"Were you about to say something?"

My gaze meets hers again.

"You were going to apologize for last night, weren't you?"

I shrug.

"Can I ask you something?"

"Okay."

"Are you sorry you kissed me?"

"No." I don't have to think about it. Kissing Harmony might just be the best spontaneous thing I've ever done. "I'm not sorry I kissed you, but I'm sorry that I didn't ask you first."

"I'm not," she says, pulling the blanket tighter around her. "Because I might have overthought it, and it was perfect just the way it was."

I feel the heat flush through my body. Am I blushing? I never blush, or I didn't used to anyway. Still, I agree, it was perfect. Before I can tell her, there's a muffled bark at the back door. Shit, I forgot my dog.

Rushing to the back door, I open it to a snow-covered, giant, angry-looking yellow dog. I swear he sneers at me as he pushes past into the kitchen. His demeanor turns pathetic as he moves to Harmony to rest his frozen head on her leg.

"Poor baby, are you frozen?" she coos. Did he just smirk at me? "Come here. I'll share my blanket with you." She slides to the floor and wraps the blanket around the dog.

"Seriously?"

"I'm not the one so busy thinking about kissing the girl again that I left my dog outside in the snow." Okay, fair point. "You're not thinking that at all are you, big boy," she says, ruffling his ears. "Because you're a good boy."

I think the noise I make is something that combines a snort, a grunt, and a guffaw. She pretends to ignore me, but I see the corners of her mouth tick up.

"You're baiting me."

She shrugs, and I swear to all that is fucking holy, it is the sexiest shrug I've ever seen. Without thinking, I push the dog away, wrap my arms around her and pick her up. The second her ass meets the table, I'm between her legs with my lips pressed against hers.

Her arms close around my neck as my tongue chases hers. Opening the blanket, I pull her against me on the edge of the table. The aching bulge in my jeans presses against a pair of shorts that barely covers her. Jesus, I'm not this strong. Her hands drift down my shirt until they can pull the hem up to rest on my stomach.

"Harmony," I warn.

"I know," she whispers against my lips. "I know," she says stronger the second time and straightens her back.

I step back, helping her off the table. Finding the edges of the blanket, she pulls it back around her, covering straining nipples begging for my touch. That image does nothing to curb my raging erection.

"I'm going to get dressed," she adds before turning toward her bedroom.

"Good. Yeah." My brain can't think of anything else. I start the monotonous routine of making breakfast hoping it will calm me down.

By the time I have the oatmeal ready, she's returned. "I hope you'll eat this. I've got stuff to put on it." She sits at the table and begins to eat. I can think of so many more things that table should be used for than eating. Well, eating oatmeal anyway.

"Are we still checking on your neighbors?" she asks.

"Yeah, they're older. I don't like the thought of something happening over there and no one knowing about it."

"Sounds good." We both sound like we're trying to force a conversation that would have come easily earlier. Her side of it would have anyway. Maybe we could use some fresh air. "Are we still taking the horses?"

"I thought we would." She nods her head and continues eating. I can't think of a single thing to say so we eat in silence until we've finished.

"Ready?" I ask after the dishes are drying in the rack. Digging out a handful of winter gear, she tries on different coveralls until she finds a pair that fits the closest. I add gloves, hat, and face covering to her look.

"I feel like that kid from *A Christmas Story*. I really can't put my arms down."

"At least you'll be warm." I lead her and Reacher out the front door. She steps off the porch and into snow that reaches her knees. I noticed when I let the dog out that we had new snow on the ground. "You okay?"

"Peachy," she says, pulling a boot out of the drift. Together, we finally make it to the barn. I sit her on a bale of hay to warm up while I saddle the horses. They're both snorting and stamping in the frigid air. Reacher races around digging in the snow like he might find buried treasure.

"This is Hoss," I tell her when I'm finished saddling my big roan gelding. "And this is Joe," I add, pointing to the small bay she's going to ride. I hook a lead line to his bridle so I can still control him from my horse.

"*Bonanza*?" she asks.

I shrug a shoulder and help her onto Joe.

"You remember I've never ridden before, right?" She has a death grip on the saddle horn.

"Don't worry, I've got you." Holding both the lead line and my reins, I swing onto Hoss. With a whistle at Reacher, we head out of the barn.

"Wow, it's cold out here."

"Do you want to change your mind?"

"No," she answers, straightening her shoulders. "I'll be fine."

She is too. It takes us half an hour to ride the mile, but she never complains. Her only concession to the cold is to keep her mouth closed most of the way.

I'll admit that I miss her banter as we slog through the snow. It's not possible to fall for someone in a day, is it? Can you feel this connected to someone who you know basically nothing about?

I knew a few things about Harmony Ellis before she walked into my kitchen yesterday. I already knew she was the nice sister. Any time I saw her with Travis in high school, she was laughing. I also know she has a voice that can tame even the most savage beast. At graduation, she was in the top ten percent of the class. She had as many cords around her neck in her gown as Travis, which was substantial.

She can cook, that's for damn sure. The gumbo last night was orgasmic. I should probably think about something other than orgasms. Anyway, she's gorgeous, funny, and kind. What else do I need to know about her? How about the sounds she makes when she comes on my cock? Jesus. Good thing it's freezing.

"Is that it?" she asks, pointing to a plume of smoke coming from a distant chimney.

"That's it." We arrive at the house, and I help Harmony off the horse.

"Oh my, look what the weather blew in." Mr. Harris stands in his front door. He quickly rushes us inside before taking our horses to his barn. I help Harmony unwrap from the layers of clothing she's in.

"Are you trying to freeze your guest, Beau?" Mrs. Harris asks. "She's as cold as ice. Come here, sugar. You sit down while I make some hot tea." She gives me a shake of her head before turning to the stove. Reacher, who's kept up with us the entire trip, makes himself comfortable in front of the fireplace next to their dog.

"Hi, I'm Harmony."

"I know who you are, honey. We watched every episode of that country star show you were on. Nate and I were so proud when you won."

"Who were we proud of?" Nate asks, stepping into the kitchen.

"You remember the youngest Ellis girl," she chastises. "I was telling her about watching that show she was on. I'm

Reba," she adds. "Like the star, but without the singing voice."

"We thought we would come see how you're holding up in the snow," I try.

"We're just fine," Reba answers as the kettle begins to whistle. "But the bigger question is, what are you doing at Beau's?" She sets a cup of tea in front of Harmony and sits in a chair across from her. I'm pretty sure I'll be hearing about this for a while to come. I should have thought this venture out better.

"I was heading home for the holidays and got trapped in the storm."

"Oh, bless your heart. It's a good thing you got stranded near his place then," Reba answers. Sure, that's what we'll go with. Not the story about how my brother abandoned her in my guest bedroom.

"Speaking of, we wanted to ask if you had any extra Christmas lights for our tree?" Harmony asks.

"Beau put up a tree?" Reba asks as if the very concept is an aberration. She and Nate exchange looks before looking at me. I ignore them. "Of course we have extra lights. We'll dig them out after you warm up a little."

"We might be experiencing a Christmas miracle, Mother," Nate teases.

"All right." There's no need to point out what an asshole I've been in the past so blatantly.

"We're just giving you a hard time. Come on, let's go find the extra lights," Reba said, patting Harmony on the leg. We watch them leave the kitchen for another part of the house.

"Pretty girl," Nate says.

"She is," I agree.

"Might be worth keeping."

"She's one of Travis's friends," I argue. "I don't even know her. She just got trapped here because of the snow."

"Still," he says. "No time like the present. To get to know someone that is." There's a smirk on his face that makes me uncomfortable. I'm saved by Harmony bouncing back into the room clutching a sack of stuff to her chest.

"Look, Beau!" she blurts. "We have lights, tinsel, some craft stuff for making more ornaments, and stockings." How? They weren't even gone that long.

"Who is Duke?" I ask as she holds up one of the stockings.

"It's one of our dogs long since gone," Reba answers. "I'm sure you can do something with the names."

"Or you can be Duke, and I can be...Sissy," Harmony says, holding up the other stocking.

"Do all of your dogs get stockings?" I ask.

"What can I say? Mother likes to sew," Nate says.

"Don't worry, I included one for Reacher."

"Or...Bitsy." Harmony laughs.

"Jesus," I swear under my breath.

"You watch that mouth, Mirabeau Rayburn," Reba warns.

"Mirabeau?" Harmony's eyebrows are so high, they almost disappear into her hairline.

"Don't," I warn. "We should be heading back." I stand and walk to the door to begin pulling back on all my outer layers.

"You don't want to stay for lunch?" Reba asks.

"I left something cooking at home. I just wanted to make sure you're okay and to borrow some lights. Thank you, though." Harmony joins me by the door. When she's redressed, we say our goodbyes and step outside. The wind feels colder than our ride over. She shivers next to me.

"Do you want to ride home behind me. I'll cut some of the wind. You'd be warmer," I offer.

"Okay. Mirabeau," I sigh as I take Joe's reins in my hand and swing up on Hoss. Reaching down, I pull Harmony up behind me. Reacher races around us in the snow. I whistle for him, and we start back to the ranch.

Harmony scoots as close to my back as possible before burying her face in my coat. Her arms wrap around my waist. I slide them inside my coat to help keep her hands warm.

Just the feel of her hands on me, even though there are multiple layers of clothes separating us, is enough to make my heart race. My mind drifts to thoughts of her heart pressed against me as we fight our way through the snow. My body heats at the feel of hers tucked against mine. This is going to be a very long ride.

seven

HARMONY

THAT WAS the longest ride ever. I know it was the same distance coming back that it was going, but something about being snuggled up behind Beau made me want to be home snuggled up to him on the couch. He kept me warm the entire trip with his strong, taut body. Of course, my mind ran wild the entire time about the shame of having so many articles of clothing separating us.

"Are you hungry?" He wraps his elbow in mine and lowers me to the ground in front of the house. "It should be ready. If you want to dish it up, I'll put the horses up."

"Sounds good." Sounds domestic.

When I push open the front door I'm hit with the most delicious aroma. Quickly, I shed all the outer layers and head for the kitchen. Sitting on the back burner simmering away is a huge pot of stew. I stir it with a spoon sitting on the spoon rest and find meat and so many different vegetables, I don't understand where he found some of them.

This meal is going to need some biscuits. Finding the ingredients, I mix some up and pop them in the oven. They're almost done when the door opens, and Reacher comes bounding into the kitchen. He sniffs the air before flopping down on his pillow.

"You made biscuits," Beau announces, bending down to peer into the oven.

"What? You're kidding," I tease in fake shock. He rolls his eyes at me. They're done, so I pull them out of the oven while he dishes out the stew. We settle at the table to eat.

"So," I say, drawing out the word. "Are we going to talk about the elephant in the room? Mirabeau?"

There's a growl from the other side of the table. He meets my gaze with a scowl. I beat my eyelashes at him until he sighs. He stalls by shoveling a massive spoonful of stew into his mouth. It's so hot, he has to drink about half of his water after. Finally, he caves.

"My mom was a history buff; especially Texas history. My brother got William Travis, hero of the Alamo. I, however, got saddled with Mirabeau Lamar. He was the second president of Texas. Couldn't name me Sam Houston after the first president and hero at San Jacinto. Nope. I got Mirabeau."

"Did they announce your entire name at graduation?" Now I'm just trying to rile him up.

"I told Principal Hamby I'd burn the school down if he did."

"I don't know. Mirabeau has a nice ring to it."

"Only a few people know my full name. They've been sworn to secrecy on penalty of death."

"You mean women don't scream Mirabeau in ecstasy?" He sets his spoon down and studies me for a minute.

"I'll make an exception for you," he growls. This conversation went sideways fast. What is wrong with me that I can't stop making veiled sexual innuendos? Or in this case, not so veiled ones.

"I think I'll just stick with Beau," I stutter.

"As long as you're screaming it, I'm good either way."

"Honey?" I say, snatching up the little bear off the table.

"Yes, sweetheart?" he teases back.

"Beau!"

"Yes, like that. Only louder and moanier." He grins across the table at me. "I'm teasing."

"I know," I snap back. It's hard to pull off indignation when my face is blazing red. Problem is, I can totally envision screaming his name while I'm pinned under him. Or over him. I'm good either way. He continues to smile as he scoops another spoonful into his mouth.

"Are you going with me to check the cattle, or are you staying here?" How does he go from flirty banter one minute to all business the next? I'm still looking for that old-fashioned fan for my face, and he doesn't even miss a beat. I wish I could learn to be that casual about it.

I have men come on to me all the time, even get an occasional inappropriate proposal. Most of my adult life I've had someone to act as a buffer. This time, though, I'm on my own. Unfortunately, left to my own devices, I fall back into my go to when I'm nervous. I start to yammer.

"No, I think I'll stay inside. Those Christmas decorations aren't going to hang themselves. I need to string the lights first, then assemble some more ornaments to complement our snowflakes, not to mention the icicles. You know, you can't just throw those up all willy-nilly. Each one needs to be placed carefully."

I stop when I notice Beau grinning at me again. "Stop. You're making me nervous," I whine. Not a good sound coming out of my mouth.

"Then my work here is done." In one perfect move, he stands, bends over to kiss my forehead, and sweeps the bowls up from the table. I might be fangirling a little bit.

"I'll get those," I say as I push up from the table. "You cooked, I'll clean."

"That would be great. Maybe I can get back before it turns dark." He stands next to the sink as we stare across the small kitchen at each other. Then he's stepping up to me. His lips meet mine, and I melt against him. I know it seems silly to get so worked up over something as simple as a kiss, but damn that man can light me up like no one has before.

His tongue sweeps against mine. My hands act on their own curling into the front of his shirt. This kiss makes me want to throw caution to the wind. Forget that I'm only here a short time. It makes me want to fall into his arms and never let go. Sadly, he steps back. I release the front of his shirt as he smiles.

"I'll be back soon." He walks to the door and pulls on his outerwear. With his hand on the door, he stops. "Maybe we can pick up where we left off." With a grin, he walks into the snow.

I stand in the door between the kitchen and mudroom staring after him like a deer in the headlights. Shaking myself from my sex stupor, I look over where Reacher is sprawled on his pillow.

"Okay. So. Christmas." The dog opens one eye in acknowledgment. He's going to be of no help. That's fine. I have plenty to keep me busy.

* * *

BEAU

To say it's cold outside would be an understatement. It's colder than when we got back at lunch. I understand that we have winter, but it's the Texas hill country, not the Arctic. At least I have an enclosed tractor to put out hay and drag the feed trailer around with.

That kiss also goes a long way to keep me warm. I love how she throws herself into kissing me back every time.

"Hey, boys," I say, walking into the barn. Pulling the horse blankets off a rack, I carry them into the stall. I've left the doors open so they can wander outside if they want. The fact they're both huddled inside one of the stalls means that's the last thing they want. I clip the blankets on both of them and toss more hay in the mangers.

"So you've both met her now." I move on to scooping out some grain from the bin. "What do you think? Am I way out of my league?" They both snort in the cold air as I fill the bunks hanging on the side of the stalls. "Yeah, I thought that's what you'd say."

I take a few minutes to scoop out some of the manure they've gifted me with. It would be nice if you could house-break a horse.

"See, the problem is she deserves everything Nashville can give her. She's a star, and I'm...well, I'm just some guy she got stuck with in a snowstorm." I close the barn door and turn to look at the house.

"Man, I'd really like to be a part of her world though. Even if just for a little while." Walking to the other side of the barn, I pull open the door where I store the tractor. I climb in and drive to the hay barn.

I know I told Harmony I'd be back before dark, but it's well past that by the time I pull the tractor back into the barn. It was a struggle to work through the snow to put the hay out. Then, I had to find the cattle to feed. I don't like making them come out of the cover in the draws to eat. It's important they maintain their body heat, so I went to them.

Closing the barn door, I walk around the corner to the house. The Christmas tree glittering in the front windows brings me to a stop. She's done an amazing job. I'm not surprised. I'm positive she's amazing at anything she sets her mind to.

But it's the first time I've seen a tree lit in those windows since my brother left. Mom would love what she's done. I can almost hear her lecturing me about the importance of traditions. But what good are traditions when there's no one to share them with?

Stepping inside, I pause to take in the transformation of what used to be my home. Harmony looks up from where she's curled up on the couch under a blanket. Her face tells me she's waiting to see what I think, and if I'm smart, it will be a glowing review.

The tree is sparkling in the soft light. It's covered in homemade ornaments woven between our snowflakes. They're all shapes, sizes, and colors.

The mantel over the fireplace is covered in silver branches she must have found around the house. Where the silver paint came from, I have no idea. She's balanced brightly colored balls that look like pieces of candy among the branches. Attached to the mantel are five stockings with the correct names on them. She's even made one for Travis and his boyfriend.

A table runner I haven't seen in a long time covers the coffee table. She's dug out every candlestick and candle my mother owned to create a festive scene down the middle. She's even made an impressive construction paper representative of mistletoe which hangs in the doorway between the living room and kitchen.

"Wow," I murmur. Her gaze follows me cautiously as I work my way around the room, taking it all in. "You've been busy."

"Is that good or bad?"

"No, it's good. Looks very...festive."

"Don't injure yourself with your enthusiasm."

"Stunning, brilliant, it's a pantheon of Christmas extravagance. Is that better?" I ask, trying to hide a smile.

"Much," Harmony says, not bothering to hide hers. She hits me with that brilliant smile I've come to crave. "Do you really like it?"

"I really do." Her smile grows a few degrees brighter. "What smells so good?"

"Oh, I found everything to make a little something for supper. You eat chicken cacciatore, don't you?"

"Just a little something, huh?" Pulling her off the couch, I wrap my arms around her. She pushes up on her toes to meet me as I bend for a kiss.

My lips are still cold when they meet hers. It doesn't matter though when a soft moan washes over me. Her small fists grip the side of my shirt pulling me closer. Spinning us, I sit on the couch pulling her onto my lap. Her thighs straddle mine.

"Where did you learn these moves," she purrs.

"Making them up as I go." Her hands slap my chest when I slide her to me. Then they wrap around my neck. My hands cup her ass pressing her against my growing length.

Our mouths press together, and this time I'm the one

moaning. She grinds her heat against me, and my tongue pushes inside her mouth. It's been a very long time since I made out on a couch. I forgot how incredible it could be. Especially with Harmony straddling my lap.

eight

HARMONY

I CAN'T BELIEVE we were interrupted by the kitchen timer. This was the first make-out session I've had since I was a teenager. Based on the hard chub pressing against me, Beau was enjoying it as much as I was.

We've been cockblocked by simmering chicken. He suggested we let it burn, but I'm pretty sure catching the house on fire is not the best option in a snowstorm.

"I don't think anything else will fit," Beau says, patting his stomach.

"Not even some gingerbread I made for dessert?"

"Jesus, Harmony. Later? After this settles?"

"Fine."

"I'm going to gain twenty pounds while you're here."

"I said fine, don't keep nagging." I stand from the table to take our dishes to the sink.

His words make me sad. While I'm here. That's just it, I'll have to go home soon, and all of this will just be a wonderful memory of how I spent Christmas. I'll have to leave Beau and Reacher to return to reality. Reality is over-rated. Reality truly does bite.

"I'm not nagging," Beau says, kissing my neck. I didn't hear him walk up behind me. At first, I'm startled, but then he wraps his strong arms around me, and I settle against his chest. "And I don't really mind putting on weight if it's because of your cooking."

"I think you're making that up. I don't feel anything but hard abs and tight glutes," I say, running my hands under his shirt. They graze across his stomach before copping a handful of his ass. Quickly, they return to his back. That ass is lethal.

"Thanks for noticing," he teases. "You know, you're getting much better at the flirting thing." I'm pushing up on my toes to kiss him when we're suddenly plunged into darkness.

"Shit. Wait right here." He moves away from me, and I hear a drawer open. A light from a flashlight illuminates the floor in front of me. "Let me find the lanterns." He leaves the kitchen but returns a few minutes later carrying several battery-operated lanterns.

"What happened?" I ask. "I mean, obviously the electricity has gone off. But why?"

"The weather earlier said to expect ice." He moves into the living room. I find him looking through the panes in the front door. "Everything is coated in ice. It's really howling out there. I'm sure it's wiped out the lines."

"Oh my gosh," I whisper, staring out the only window not blocked by the Christmas tree. Everything glistens in the beam of Beau's flashlight. He's pulled open the door to look around. The room quickly chills in the cold air. Stepping back inside, he closes the door and jogs toward the back of the house.

"Beau?" I call, following him. He's pulling on his boots and a coat in the mudroom.

"Wait inside. I need to check the generator. It powers the fridge and freezer when the electricity goes out." He doesn't wait for me to answer before hurrying outside.

Picking up a couple of pieces of firewood, I return to the living room to wait. Reacher paces the house waiting for him to reappear too. I'm not sure which of us is more worried.

"Let's see if we can take the chill out of the air." Reacher watches me as I place the logs on the fire. "Getting toastier already." The back door slams. I jump up and hurry with Reacher by my side into the hallway.

"Here," Beau says, thrusting a space heater into my hands. "Put that one in front of the sink in the kitchen with the cabinet door open. I'll put the other one in the bathroom. Although, I'll be surprised if it doesn't freeze anyway."

I walk quickly into the kitchen. Opening the cabinet door under the sink, I set the space heater on the floor and turn it on. Doors close down the hall.

"Everything okay?" I call.

"The bedrooms have no heat. We'll have to sleep out here tonight," he says, walking into the kitchen. "The generator is about maxed out. I think we have enough wood for tonight. I'll bring some more into the living room. The mudroom is going to be freezing. The couch pulls out." He stops speaking, seeming to notice for the first time that we're now reduced to one room. "I can sleep on the floor."

"You'll freeze."

"The chair then."

"You said it pulls out?" I ask, ignoring him. We're adults, surely, we can share a pull-out couch. No one needs to freeze on a cold hard floor tonight. I pull out the cushions and grab the handle.

"Here, let me do it. It weighs a ton." He pulls the bed out and unfolds it. "I'll go grab some sheets. Get anything out of your room you need." I follow him down the hallway to my room. There are not many clothes left in my bag. I keep meaning to do a load of laundry. Pulling off my comforter, I haul it back into the living room.

"Do you have some sweats I can borrow? I'm about out of clothes," I ask.

"Yeah." He stops pulling the fitted sheet onto the mattress and walks back down the hallway. By the time he returns with an armload of clothes, I have the bed made. "You might want to take a quick shower one last time while there's hot water," he adds. "It's a gas tank, but the ignition is electric."

"I'll hurry, so you have hot water too." I take a quick shower, foregoing the shampoo so Beau has some hot water. I braid my hair, pull on a pair of his sweats, and head back into the living room. "I left you a little." He looks up from the fire and freezes. "What?"

"Nothing." His gaze shifts back to the fire.

"I know. I look like a mess."

"Don't say that," he snarls, looking back up. "I was just thinking about how beautiful you look." My heart begins to pound. "I don't think it's possible for me to see you as anything else."

Now my heart is going at it so hard I don't know how he can't see it. I don't know how to respond to a statement like that. Simply saying thanks sounds so lacking.

Beau doesn't seem to be expecting an answer, though. He turns back to the fire and adds another log. I've also never had a man say something so sweet and not wait for an answering compliment. I can feel the smile warming my entire body. He's made me feel like his words were nothing more than a statement of fact. He's made me feel like I can be okay with who I am.

"I'm going to go run through the shower," he says, pushing up to his full height.

"Don't get hurt."

"What?"

"You know...running...through the shower. Never mind," I mumble. I slump down into the chair and pull one of the blankets around me. Any minute now he should wander off down the cold hallway. Instead, he stares at me for a moment before walking over. Leaning down, he places a hand on each side of the chair.

"I love how your mind works," he says quietly into my ear. Then his lips brush against mine before he stands back up. With a wink, he turns for the bathroom.

"Your flirting game is getting really good you know," I yell.

He responds with a chuckle from down the hall. Holy smokes! The shower turns on, and I try to force the vision of water sliding over his hard body from my mind.

"This is proving harder than I thought," I tell Reacher as I massage his ears with my toes. He's lying on the floor at my feet. He puffs a breath in response.

"Maybe we need something to keep us distracted until bedtime. Whenever that is." I push up from the chair and cross to the bookshelves. There has to be something to do in this house that doesn't require electricity. Except for the obvious of course.

There's not enough light to read. I don't want to spend hours in silence doing that anyway. I've finally got him talking. I don't want to lose any ground.

Lowering to my knees, I dig around in the cabinets under the bookshelves. Why does he not have any board games? Not even Candy Land left over from childhood. I find the deck of cards from yesterday. There has to be something else under here.

I continue to dig around. There are the usual storage items—serving dishes, a few more movies, a box of CDs, and a stack of scrapbooks. Pulling one out, I lean back against the cabinet to look through it.

"Find anything good?" I jump at Beau's words only a few feet from me. I didn't hear him coming back down the hall. My gaze makes a slow perusal up his bare feet, sweatpants, and T-shirt until it lands on his face. He slides to the floor next to me. He smells so good I have to fight the urge to lean in to him.

"Sorry, I didn't mean to snoop. I was just looking for some way to kill time until bed."

"There's nothing in this house you can't see." He takes the scrapbook from me and begins leafing through the pages. "These pictures are from when my parents were dating." He flips through a few more pages. "Here we go. Mom was already pregnant with me in this one. Shh," he says, bumping against me. "Scandalous." He smiles. There's a mix of wistfulness and sadness in it.

"She was beautiful," I whisper.

"She was." He seems to shake himself out of wherever his memories have taken him. He flips the book closed and returns it under the cabinet. "I'm afraid with the electricity out our choices are books or cards."

"Cards it is then. I have an idea." I take the cards and flop onto the pull-out bed. With my legs crossed, I motion for him to join me. Reacher thinks I'm talking to him and joins me on the bed. Beau sits on the other side with his long legs stretched out in front of him. "We're going to play gin, but for every game I win I get to ask you a question and vice versa. Sort of like a cross between an icebreaker and strip poker."

"This sounds like a horrible idea."

"It'll be fun. I promise not to ask anything too crazy."

He looks at me like he doesn't believe me, but he nods. I take the cards out of the pack, shuffle them, and deal them out. He wins the cut. I organize my cards and wait for him to begin. It doesn't take long for him to win the first hand. He gathers up the cards and turns his gaze on me.

"Why did you want to spend Christmas with Travis instead of your family?" he asks.

"I told you my parents are on a cruise, and I don't really want to visit my sister for the holidays." I shrug. "Travis asked, so it sounded like the best choice. Being on your own for Christmas isn't the best choice in my opinion."

"Yeah, it's not."

"I mean," I stammer, realizing too late that being alone is how Beau spends most of his time. "It's fine if that's what you like."

"I'm not sure anyone likes it, it just is. Sometimes circumstances don't include a big happy family." He deals the cards. Since he won, I get to go first this time. Reacher stretches and moves his head to my lap. I stroke his ears as I study my cards. "You're spoiling him rotten."

"But look how happy he is." Reacher sighs. I'm choosing to believe it's a happy one. "I think you're just jealous."

"Probably," he admits. "I can guarantee, though, if I put my head in your lap you'll do more than rub my ears."

My eyes feel like they're about to pop out of my head. I'm sure the shock on my face is Oscar-worthy. Beau looks over at me and laughs. Is he just trying to knock me off my game, or is he making promises? It's giving me whiplash. I toss a card on the discard pile keeping my head down. Reacher snorts and shakes his head.

"Sorry," I tell him. I guess the death grip I had on his ear wasn't working for him. So much for my ally in this. Beau chuckles again and throws a card. "It's not going to work you know. You're not going distract me from winning."

"What? Me?" he says, acting offended. "Surely not." What's frustrating is, he wins anyway.

"Who was your first?" he asks.

"Wow, going straight for the jugular. How do you know there's even a first?" I ask. His eyes fire for a second with something I can't quite place. Lust? Jealousy? Hunger? "Let's see. I was seventeen. It was prom night with Chase Hansen. Cliché, right?"

"Not cliché. Not very exciting either." He shuffles the cards and deals them.

"Well, he was a senior, so I thought it was exciting at the time."

"Was he your boyfriend."

"For about two minutes. He was a nice guy though. Could have been worse." I pick up my cards. Not too bad a hand. This time I can win. I can't be the only one in this room sharing her darkest secrets. I need to even the score.

nine

BEAU

I KNEW this was a bad idea when she suggested it. Not that I don't want to know everything about her because I do. Every single detail. My life, however, is boring. She's never going to look back once she gets to know me. I have nothing to hide, except maybe monotony.

Harmony wins the next hand. Even without seeing the cards, I would know based on the wiggly happy dance she does.

"Okay, let me see." She's adorable. I scowl at her anyway. "Who was your first?" I grimace, this is a horrible story. More embarrassing than anything.

"It's even more cliché than yours. I was nineteen. Travis was at a sleepover. I went to the bar out on the highway, got drunk, and wound up in a hotel room with someone I think was just going through. I remember her name was Janet."

"That's horrible," she says. Her big blue eyes gaze at me without judgment. That's at least something. I'm judging me. Who does that? "I figured you had all the girls in high school you could wish for."

"I was too busy studying, playing sports, and working here to have time to date. I was totally focused on getting into college."

"I understand that. I've been so focused on my singing career that it doesn't leave much time for anyone else. It's been ages since I've been on a date, much less been in a relationship with anyone.

People think I have my pick of the gorgeous men in Nashville. Except, I'm always surrounded by people needing something. My agent, my assistant, my label, even my parents are always wanting something."

I feel the scowl return to my face. I wish she would elaborate on what her parents always want from her, but I don't feel like it's my place to ask. I never knew them, but I saw them occasionally on the television next to her. I know they hightailed it out of Dansboro Crossing for greener pastures the moment their daughter got her first contract.

It wouldn't surprise me if the cruise they're on was funded by Harmony. Her generosity is apparent in everything she does. Instead of asking though, I wait for her to deal the cards.

"What is your favorite song you wrote?" I ask when I win. I decided to take this game down a notch. There's no way I want to upset her.

"I think it's the one I'm working on right now," she answers. "Did I tell you it started forming last night? I even have a few words." She hums a few bars. "Uhh, I can't wait until it's out of my head and on paper."

"You'll get it," I assure her. She will too. I have no doubt.

"Can I ask you something? I know I've only won one game, but it's something I've been wondering about since

I've been here." Her face becomes sober as she waits for an answer.

"Okay," I say warily. It could be anything.

"I heard you got all these scholarships to go to college. They said you had early admittance to Yale. Why didn't you go?"

I consider her question for several minutes. There are a number of reasons I stayed here. I've never discussed them with anyone before. Not even the counselor I hired for Travis after our parents' death. I don't think anyone's ever thought to ask anyway.

"Because this was Travis's home," I begin. "He deserved to stay here. I didn't want to drag him away from the only thing he knew."

"Have you ever regretted it?"

"No." I don't have to think about it. "Harmony, look at me." I wait until her gaze meets mine. "No, I've never regretted even a moment of my decision. He got to stay in his school with friends who accepted him for who he is. I'll never regret giving that to him. And I like it here." I look around the house as if it will agree with me.

"But—"

"No but, Harmony," I snap. "I don't need my decisions second-guessed." It comes out harsher than I intended. She grows quiet as I gather up the cards and toss them on the coffee table. "I think I'm going to turn in. I need to check water tomorrow."

I toss another couple of logs on the fire and climb on the bed. Harmony settles on the farthest edge from me facing away. I really should apologize.

Suddenly, she's pushed against my back. She begins to giggle. I sit up and look at what she's so tickled about.

Reacher covers most of her half of the bed forcing her onto mine. "Sorry," she says.

"Reacher!" I growl. He ignores me. I scowl at her, but she starts laughing again. With a sigh, I lay back down. "I guess we'll stay warm."

"Beau? I'm sorry." I know she's not talking about the dog this time. I roll over until I'm facing her.

"My fault. I don't know why I get so angry when anything about that is brought up."

"I think because it's so hard to understand how something so bad could happen." She cups my cheek in her hand. "I'm so sorry you lost them. That you had to make those decisions so young. I hope Travis knows what you gave up for him." Her lips press against mine, and the knot in my chest loosens a little.

She grips the front of my shirt and rolls me onto her as our kiss deepens. Jesus, I'm desperate to make love to this woman. To slip into her warmth and claim her. To never let her go. I stop, though, because it's only going to make her leaving harder. And I don't want either of us hurt.

"Harmony," I whisper. I don't know if I'm begging or warning.

"I know," she says. I roll off her and face away once again. She presses her body against mine. It'll have to do for now.

* * *

HARMONY

Bright light spears through my eyelids. Slowly I open them to find the sun streaming through the windows not blocked by the tree. It's the first bright and sunny day I've seen since I came here.

I clamp my eyes closed again refusing to leave the warm nest I'm curled up in. Where am I? I open one eye and look around. Beau is sitting in the chair with a large sketch pad on his lap.

"Good morning," I rasp.

"Mmm," he grunts, bent over his pencil. Reacher walks over and licks my face. At least someone's happy to see me this morning.

"What are you doing?" I ask.

"Working on something." Thank you, Captain Obvious.

"Anything interesting?" He shrugs. So much for witty morning reparte.

"Do we have electricity yet?" I try again.

"No."

"How about is the bathroom still working?" He puts his pencil down and looks at me. His scowl smooths into a smile. That's better.

"The water hasn't frozen, but there's no hot water left."

"No using a bucket at least."

"Not yet."

The mere image of me squatting over a bucket makes me shudder. I throw the covers back and climb off the bed. Somehow, I managed to pull my fuzzy socks off in the middle of the night. He holds them out to me. I slide them on before standing.

It's not as cold in the room as I thought it would be. The fire crackles as I stretch my limbs. It's been a long time since I've slept on a pull-out couch. They never get any more comfortable.

The bathroom isn't horrible. The little space heater is working its guts out trying to keep the pipes from freezing.

It does nothing, however, to warm the toilet seat. Would have been nice if he'd warned me about that. Then again, he's a man. He probably just peed out the front door. I wonder if it freezes?

Lord, I might have to read a book today. My intelligent thoughts seem to be leaving me in droves. I finish and hurry back to the living room.

"Hold on," I say, coming to a stop halfway through the room. "When did the presents show up?" There are a handful of packages sitting under the tree. I think I'd remember if they were there last night. Although I was pretty focused on how sexy his bare feet are. I could have missed them.

"How long have you been awake?" I ask.

He shrugs.

"Were you watching me sleep the whole time?" Another shrug. "Creeper."

"Hey, you're in my house. Fair game." It's my turn to shrug. I guess he makes a good point there.

"Where did these come from?" I move closer to the tree. There are a couple labeled with Travis and still more with Trace and Reacher. Trace is Travis's boyfriend. Based on the fact Beau bought him Christmas presents, they must be serious.

Looking closer, I find a couple with my name on them. Shit! Why didn't I think about grabbing a few gifts on the way here. Because I thought I'd have time to do some shopping later is why.

"How?" I begin spinning around to ask how he managed to buy me something. Instead of answering, he thrust a large mug of hot chocolate into my hand. He's even put whipped cream on top and peppermint in it. Once I've taken it, he returns to the kitchen. A few minutes later he returns with leftover coffee cake.

"How what?" he asks, settling back in the chair.

"How did you go shopping?" I sit back on the opened bed again. Reacher sits next to me hoping for a piece of cake. I break off a small bite for him. Beau huffs but says nothing. I think he's given up when it comes to me and his dog.

"Who says I went shopping?" he answers.

"I guess no one?" He smiles as he cuts a piece of cake with his fork. His eyes twinkle with mischief. Hmm, that starts my wheels turning. "Are you going to give me a hint?"

"About what?"

"The presents, what else?" I say in exasperation.

"Nope."

"Uhhh, you're so obnoxious." His eyebrows shoot up in surprise. "It won't kill you to give me one hint." Now his face relaxes back to amusement. When did I get to read Beau Rayburn's expressions so well? "Is it animal, vegetable, or mineral?"

"Well, I'm not wrapping up an animal for twenty-four hours before it's opened."

"Twenty-four hours!" I shout a little too loudly. Reacher picks his head up to stare at me from the end of the bed. "We could open them now. No one's going to know we didn't wait until officially Christmas Day. It'll be our little secret." Beau continues to eat without saying a word.

"At least let me shake them," I beg. "I bet I can guess based on one shake. I've done it before. I used to shake the crap out of our presents as a kid."

Chewing slowly, his gaze flicks up to mine then back down to the cake. I have the sudden urge to slap that plate out of his hands.

"My sister used to unwrap hers early to see what they were," I continue. "She'd rewrap them so Mom never knew. She hates surprises. I bet your family didn't even open them on Christmas. I bet you waited until after."

"We're not barbarians," he says. I blow out a breath. My cake remains hardly touched as I change tactics.

"You know," I say, pushing up on my knees to face him. "I could let you unwrap an early present too." I'm doing my best to be sexy.

"You're trading sex for a shake of a present?"

"Okay, fine. No." I slump back down on the couch. Picking up my food, I take angry bites of it.

Does he not understand how much I love Christmas? We always got to pick out one present to unwrap on Christmas Eve. It made the torture worth waiting to unwrap the rest the next day. Parents can be so cruel. So can sexy, single men apparently.

"Is this you throwing a tantrum?"

"Maybe," I answer.

"How about this," he says. "How about I keep you occupied all day so you don't think about those presents?"

"Sounds like a reasonable plan. How?"

"I have to check water today. You can go with me. We'll take the tractor, so you'll have to sit on my lap, but you'll be warm. It's bright and sunny today. We might can build a snowman if you're good."

"Yeah?"

"Yeah," he says, standing. Bending over, he boops my nose. "But you have to be good." Sweeping up the plates and mugs, he walks into the kitchen. I have to be good, huh. Just how good do I have to be? I think I'm starting to prefer naughty.

ten

BEAU

IT'S STILL FREEZING OUTSIDE. I left Harmony to dress while I refilled the generator with fuel. She joined me to stack extra firewood in the mudroom. She had already moved the warm wood to the living room by the time I brought the first bundle over from the barn. I was smarter this time and fashioned a sled out of an old door to drag it over on. Four loads, and there is enough to heat the house for a while.

I decide to leave Reacher in the house. There is definitely not enough room in the tractor for all of us. Harmony is adorable in her oversized coveralls. She really does look like that kid from the movie with her arms held away from her body in the snow.

I start the tractor to warm it up then haul her inside. It's not the easiest task with both of us completely ensconced in outerwear.

Once we're both inside, I slide onto the seat and back the tractor out of the barn. I shift it to start forward and wrap an arm around her waist. Gently, I lower her to my left leg. It won't be easy to shift, but I don't care. Something seems right having her with me. Like she belongs here.

"Are you okay?" I ask.

"I'm good. It's beautiful, isn't it?"

"It is," I agree. It's all beautiful—her, the landscape, everything. "Tell me if you get tired."

"Okay. What do you have to do again?"

"Check if the ice needs to be broken on the water so the cattle can drink. I'll have to get out, but you can wait in here where it's warm."

It doesn't take long to reach the first water trough. I put the tractor in idle and climb down. Pulling the axe out from next to the seat, I set about working on the ice. Harmony watches me from her warm seat in the tractor. There are cattle standing around waiting for a drink.

"Can I do one?" she asks when I'm done. We jockey around until she's sitting on my leg again.

"Only if you promise not to chop your foot off."

"I won't if I have a good teacher."

I catch myself smiling. I do that a lot suddenly. She's a mess, but if she wants to get out in the cold and hack at some ice, who am I to deny her.

At the next trough, she climbs out but simply stands aside to watch how I use the axe. By the next one, though, she's ready.

"Okay. Wide stance." She spreads her feet apart. "Make sure you're steady." She does some kind of wiggle like she's teeing up on the golf course. "Don't swing it too high to start. Just take baby swings."

She nods and picks the axe up to waist level. With a roar that would make a warrior princess proud, she brings it down with a resounding whack.

It takes longer than if I did it, but eventually she makes it through the ice. Holding the axe in the air, she does another yell. This time, though, it makes my ears burn in surprise.

"Yes. Fuck everyone who said I'd never be more than a mindless voice," she announces. It's the first fuck I've heard her utter. It's adorable and a total shock at the same time.

"Damn, Xena. Next time I'll let you chop wood. That should even grow some hair on your chest."

"Well, let's not get too carried away," she says. "Don't want to have to wax my chest." She takes the axe in both hands and shakes it over her head with another roar.

"Okay, come on." I take the axe in one hand and toss her over my shoulder with the other. "You have at least five more to do." I set her on the steps of the tractor.

"Oh, my. Look who's doing the manhandling now," she teases.

"Behave, or there'll be more."

"Ooh, I don't think I want to behave now." Jesus. Thoughts of sex in the seat of my tractor flood my mind. I've never had sex in a tractor, but I'm liking the idea. "Come here."

She's almost my height standing on the step. I pull her to me and press my lips to hers. She moans as she pulls me closer. My tongue sweeps inside her mouth. She tastes of chocolate, the mint from her toothpaste, and brown sugar. I want more. I want all of her.

The kiss breaks, and she tugs me into the cab. I'm pushed onto the seat as she climbs up to straddle my lap. Her hands grapple with the buttons on my coat, finally pulling it off over my head. It's tossed on the floor as her mouth crashes back against mine. She has on a full piece coverall. I snag the zipper between my fingers and pull it down her body.

Harmony stands and tugs her boots off. Then she shimmies from the open suit keeping her warm. Leaning forward, I turn the heater up. I want to know that her shivers aren't caused by the cold.

Quickly, I push the shoulder straps on my suit down and push it to my ankles. My boots are a little harder to get off. Doesn't matter anyway. She's back on my lap in a snap with her tongue in my mouth.

Bare hands slide under my shirt, tugging it off my body. The floor of the tractor is slowly filling with our clothes. She sits back to take a lust-fueled gaze at my body. I can still feel her hands on me from the first time we met in the kitchen. I want that feeling again. She obliges by running her palms up my chest.

"Beau." It comes out in a plea. I slide her shirt up her torso until it's added to the pile. She sits on my lap in nothing but a bra and a pair of pants. My knuckle blazes its way down her breastbone to her stomach.

"Jesus." My mind says a thousand things to her. It speaks of how gorgeous she is, how I want her so bad I'm shaking, how lucky I am that she's here. But it can't form the words for any of those.

"Yeah," she says seeming to understand. "Do you think this will break us?" she whispers. I'd like to say no, that nothing will ever hurt us. It will. This will absolutely break us, but I no longer care.

I lean forward just enough to reach around her. Her bra slides off her shoulders. My hand slides down her body again blazing a fire.

I press her to me until she's kneeling high enough for me to draw one of her taught nipples between my lips. Her back arches encouraging me to continue. I don't want to disappoint so I lavish it with my tongue until she squirms.

My focus moves to the other one next. I love the way she moans my name when I tug at the nub. I brand everything she loves in my memory. I slide my hand under her jeans finding her soaked. All for me. My fingers play with her, caressing between her entrance and clit.

"These need to go," I growl, tugging my hand out. She rockets off my lap to wiggle from her jeans. Then her hands go to work on mine. "I don't have any condoms."

"I'm on birth control," she answers. I know neither of us have done this in a long time, so I'm not worried about catching anything. I need to remember and go slow though. As much as I want to leave her sore and knowing who made her that way, I don't want her hurt.

She manages to work my jeans free. I push them to my ankles. She takes one look at me sitting on the seat in nothing but my underwear and half my outwear at my ankles and smiles.

"We can do better than that." She slides both hands inside my boxer briefs and slides them down. My length stands proudly waiting for her. She slides out of her panties and eases back onto my lap. She doesn't wait for me to go slow, instead she lines herself up and slides down. She's the best thing I've felt in a long time. Possibly ever.

"Ride me hard, princess," I say.

She grins and raises back up on her knees before slamming back down.

"Come on. Use it like you own it."

She repeats her motion carefully a couple more times before I sink my hands onto her ass.

"You're fucking like a schoolgirl. Let me show you how to fuck like a rock star."

I guide her up and down in a hard, punishing pace. When she takes over, I flip my hand to press against her clit again.

"Beau," she chants. That's what I like to hear.

"Make me come, gorgeous." I slap her ass just for emphasis. She looks shocked for a beat before her eyes heat with pleasure. So, she acts sweet but likes rough. I can do that.

Pulling her off my lap, I spin her until her hands are pressed against the back window. Pushing back inside her, I slam into her as she begs for more.

"Come for me, siren." I reach around and pinch her clit between my finger and thumb. It does the trick.

"Beau," she screams as she comes apart. She clamps my dick in a vise grip as she comes around me. I can't hold the heat at bay. It winds up my spine until I'm spilling inside of her.

"Take it all," I moan as I thrust one last time. Her hands move from the window to the back of the seat as I pull her up to me. I ease out so her feet can reach the floor. Spinning us back around, I collapse on the seat with her on my lap. "Fuck."

"Yeah," she says in a muffled voice. "We did." Her face is buried against my neck as I hold her close. Our chests heave in unison fighting for breath. My heart races like I've raced a marathon. But over it all, I have the most overwhelming feeling of peace. Like this is where I've meant to be from the beginning. With Harmony.

I pull her face up so I can kiss her plump lips. They're a little burned looking from my stubble. I didn't get to shave this morning. Wait until I use those rough cheeks on the inside of her thighs.

"So, that happened," she says.

"It did," I agree.

"No regrets."

"None." She relaxes against me. I'm glad I turned the heater up earlier, though the windshield is now covered in condensation. It makes a private cocoon we can relax in for a little while.

"I have a question." Her soft gaze turns to mine. "Where did you learn to talk like that? You must drive the women wild."

"I saved it for you." She looks at me in disbelief. "Really, I've never done that before. I think I just wanted you to lose your mind." Honestly, what I really want is to ruin her. Make her so hungry for me that no other man will work. Keep her wanting more.

"You're a quick study then." I laugh. "So, first time, huh. What else was a first?"

"The tractor," I answer.

"Oh, same here."

"First time without a condom."

"Same. I have to confess, it's a little messy."

"Yeah." I laugh again. "First time I'd really like a repeat performance."

"Yeah," she says softly. "Me too."

"I guess we'd better finish with the ice so we can get back then."

"Hey, you know what?" she asks.

"What." I can't imagine what is swirling around in that brain of hers. I've found I actually like the continual banter now.

"I haven't thought about those presents in a while."

"And to think, I was just about to agree to let you open them all."

eleven

HARMONY

I AM ATTACKING this ice like my life depends on it. My sanity might very well. Beau Rayburn should come with a warning label. Ride at your own risk. I'm sore, tired, and can't wait for more. That's right, I ripped that fourth wall right down. I don't know if that's a thing, but it should be. Sex should be labeled the fourth wall. Spread the word. I just took a sledgehammer to that bitch.

"Slow down before you lose a leg," he says next to me. I know I make him nervous swinging this thing around.

"Fine, here. I'm going to go make a fucking snow angel." At least the snow should cool me off a little.

"Damn, you get a little and turn into a sailor," he teases. Taking the axe, he takes over where I left off. I flop backward into the snow. Okay, it's more like ice, but at least it's cold. I spread my legs and brush my arms in an arc. Beau stops chopping to watch me. "Now moan 'more, Beau.'" I glare at him. He just laughs and goes back to chopping.

I do several more rounds of ground calisthenics before

stopping. I'm panting from the exertion in the cold. My legs are still spread eagle while I lay on the ground. A shadow crosses over my body. Opening my eyes, I find Beau standing over me with a serious look on his face.

"Remember that pose. That's what I need from you this afternoon." I throw a fistful of snow at him. Most of it just blows back in my face. Laughing again, he reaches down to help me up. I let him pull me off the ground and into his arms. "This isn't going to get awkward, is it?"

"Doesn't seem like you're going to let it," I answer again his chest.

"Good. I don't want you regretting anything. You can put the brakes on if you want, but never regrets."

"I guess that depends on how good you are at eating pussy." A deep rumble spills up from his chest.

"Like my life depends on it," he says.

"Yeah, well, put your money where your mouth is." Is it possible to be any clearer what I'm wanting the second we walk back into that house?

"Or I can put it somewhere better."

"Your mouth?" I'm kidding, I know what he means.

"My mouth." The words still send a shiver down my body. "Are you cold?"

"Yeah, let's go with that." Who would have thought I would turn into a sex fiend. It has to be more than that. Could I be falling for Beau? Of course I am, which is going to suck when I head back to Nashville.

He moves me to the tractor and helps me up the steps. I settle back on his lap. Snuggling against him, I press kisses to his neck.

He finishes chopping up the rest of the ice while I watch from the cab. It's still cold, but at least it hasn't started snowing again. When we get back, he pulls the tractor into the barn. After helping me down, he checks on the horses.

"I can hear your stomach rumbling," he says as we walk to the house. "How does stew again sound?"

"Good." We walk in the house to Reacher's enthusiastic greeting. Beau sends him outside for a few minutes while we remove all the outer layers of clothes.

"Work on the fire, and I'll put the stew on," he says.

I toss several more logs on to take the chill out of the room. There's a bark at the door, and Reacher runs in to find me a few minutes after. We both sit by the fire to warm up.

Beau carries two bowls of stew into the living room for us. I move to the bed, and he hands me one. It's finally getting warm in here.

He takes our empty dishes to the kitchen when we're done. I can hear him putting the kettle on for dish water. It's like living in the old west. My belly is full of stew, the room is finally warm, and I can barely keep my eyes open. Kicking off my jeans, I curl up under the covers.

My mind drifts over everything that's happened since I've been here. It's crazy, but I can't remember ever being this happy. Not in a long time anyway. The last thing I feel before drifting off is the bed dip and a warm man nestle up behind me. With Beau on one side and Reacher on the other, I drift into a deep sleep.

I don't know how long I've been asleep when something pulls me from a dream. It's not an unpleasant jolt from sleep, it's more like a lovely sensation through my body. My mind floats awake. I'm lying on my back with someone between my legs. My back arches as Beau's tongue sweeps through my folds. It's a pretty damn good way to be woken up.

"Beau," I moan, sweeping the covers back. I want to see him at work. His dark gaze meets mine from between my thighs. His head lowers again as he returns to his work. I gasp when his tongue swipes over my clit. Slapping his head with my hand, I fist a handful of his hair. My hips rise off the mattress to meet his hungry mouth.

Gently, he sucks my nub between his lips, and I try to squirm away. His strong arm presses me down to hold me in place. I want to protest, it's almost too much. But my words fail me this time. There's only one word on my lips.

"Beau," I pant. A thumb takes over as his tongue slides inside me. I don't know if it's the new sensation or his rumbling growl that makes me let go.

I float through waves as my mouth opens in a silent scream. I want more while at the same time needing less. He brings me down slowly until I'm nothing more than bones spread on the bed. His lips place a soft kiss on my stomach.

"Beau," I sigh this time.

"I like how you say my name." His head rests on my abdomen. My hand runs through his soft hair, a little more gently this time. We lay still simply enjoying being together. I know it can't last. I have a tour to complete, and he has a ranch to run. But, for right now, I can pretend. I can pretend this bubble is how it will always be between us.

"I should get the chores done before it gets dark," he says. He doesn't move as my hands continue raking my fingers through his hair. Finally, he sighs and pushes to his knees.

"What can I do to help?"

"Stay warm. I won't be very long." He gets off the bed. I suppress the urge to pull him back down on top of me.

"I'll have something hot for you when you get done."

I'm talking about a drink, but he shoots me a smirk. My face grows red. Before I can stammer out something stupid, he walks to the mudroom. He whistles, and Reacher follows him out.

As much as I'd love to stay here in my post sex stupor, I'm sure there's something I can do to help. I swing to a sitting position, and my gaze lands on those pesky presents under the tree. Nope, I can resist. But what am I going to do for a Christmas present for Beau. It's not like there's anything in my suitcase he'd want.

I pull one of the blankets around me when I stand up. Maybe I can find inspiration somewhere in this house. After a quick spin around the living room, I walk down the hall to his bedroom.

My hand freezes on the door handle. It will be the first time I'll see this room, and it feels like I'm breaking a confidence. Well, I guess if he's got a stack of skinsuits in his closet, I might as well find out now.

Pushing the door open slowly, I take a look around. I don't know what I'm expecting. It looks like any man's bedroom. The furniture looks like it came from a discount store.

There's a gray comforter on the bed and a large framed black and white scenery photo over it. The only thing with much color is the large area rug in deep shades of reds, blues, and greens. Not much of inspiration in here.

There's one other place I can look. Walking around the bed, I stop in front of the nightstand. There's a book on top with a bookmark holding his place. Not a serial killer then. Everyone knows dog-earring a book is one of the signs.

I pull out the drawer on top. It's filled with what looks like the stash of an elementary kid. Keys, a video game, lube (okay, maybe not elementary), and a handful of trinkets.

Under all of it are several photos of Beau and his brother. It's the first photos I've seen of them as adults.

That gives me an idea. It's childish, but I could use some of the leftover craft supplies to make frames for his office. That wall of photos really needs updating.

I gather up the photos and close the drawer. The rest of the nightstand doesn't have much in it at all. Taking the photos, I return to the kitchen. It didn't take long to get chilled in that part of the house.

I sit at the table and dig through the art supplies. By the time Beau comes stomping back in the mudroom, I've created several frames. They're wrapped and sitting under the tree. Quickly, I turn on the stove for hot water. I hear a load of wood hit the stack.

"It's still freezing out there," he says, stepping into the kitchen. Reacher trots in behind him with his tail wagging. I automatically reach for one of the treats in the jar on the counter.

"Figured you'd bring some more wood with you?" He smirks. Oh Lord. "Go ahead and say it."

"Nah, it's too easy." I stand with my arms crossed and stare at him. His grin grows broader. "I've got your wood right here." Yeah, I set him up. I roll my eyes anyway. "Any requests for dinner?" I thrust a cup of tea into his hands.

"Anything sounds good." My stomach growls in agreement.

"How about you? You'd be good for dinner." He wraps an arm around my waist and pulls me on to his lap as he sits at the table. Somehow, he manages not to burn either of us with his tea. I can't say I disagree with his statement. I wouldn't mind being feasted on for dinner. But we can't exist on sex alone. Right?

"I'm being serious," I say.

"So am I," he counters. "Fine, you can be dessert."

We decide on making a pizza. Beau has all the ingredients, and the oven is gas. He has to practically climb in it to start the pilot light again.

He produces a pizza stone from one of the cabinets. It makes me wonder how much time he actually spends in the kitchen. I don't even have a pizza stone. Of course, I order in most of what I eat now. When it's ready, we take it into the living room and eat it while flopped on the couch.

"Last piece?" he offers.

"There's no way any more will fit in here." I lay back on the couch and rub my stomach for emphasis. "I think we're going to have to let it settle before moving onto dessert." After all, there is nothing remotely sexy about belching pizza in the middle of love making.

"Probably not a bad idea. Nothing crushes an orgasm like seeing pizza coming back up." He sets the pan with the remaining piece on the coffee table. Reacher snarfs it down in two bites. "We're not going to want him sleeping with us tonight either." The dog puffs out a round of gas and looks at us over his shoulder.

"Nice." I push up until I'm resting against the back of the pull-out couch. "What do you want to do until the pizza settles? What about another round of gin?"

Beau moans, but tosses me the cards from the coffee table anyway. I think, secretly, he likes us learning more about each other. Deep down, I think he's a romantic.

twelve

BEAU

"I GUESS I'd have to say, if I could pick anywhere to go on vacation, it would be Greece," I say. We decided to continue our card game we started last night. The questions are much tamer this time.

I agree with Harmony, it's a good way to get to know someone. I also think we're out of creative ways to keep ourselves entertained that doesn't include seeing the pizza again.

"Really. Why?"

"The water is supposed to be amazing. There's history everywhere, and the food is good." I shrug. "I don't know, just seems like a good spot."

"I agree, I've always heard it's beautiful. I think my fantasy vacation is hiking to Machu Picchu." We decided on a different format this time. Whoever wins the hand gets to ask the question, but we both answer. Makes the game go faster. "I don't know why. The pictures of it always looks like it's mystical especially the ones with the fog."

"Yeah, those are pretty cool looking. Okay, I'd tag along on that one."

"We should make a pact to do both someday." She holds out her pinkie to me.

What the hell. I loop it in mine and we "shake" on it. Sitting back, she sweeps up the cards and begins to shuffle. "You know, I've traveled all over the country singing. I never see anything except the bus windshield, hotel rooms, and venues. It would be nice to have time to see something else."

"I understand. The only time I seem to leave here is to see Travis in Austin." I don't tell her that part of that is because I haven't bothered to go anywhere in a long time. Vacationing on my own just doesn't appeal to me. Harmony in a bikini floating in the Aegean, however, sounds like heaven. I let my mind stray to all the things I could do to her on a private beach.

"Beau?"

"What?" I guess I've been daydreaming for a while now. The cards have already been dealt. I snatch mine up and organize them into runs and suites. "You know this would be much better if it was strip poker," I point out.

"I would be naked by now. I'm horrible at this."

"Exactly. That's a game I could really get behind."

"Or we could just skip the poker part," she says, batting her eyelashes at me.

"Now you're thinking." Throwing my cards over my shoulder, I grab one of her ankles and jerk her down on the bed. She squeals with laughter as I pounce.

That squeal turns into a moan as I trap her underneath me. My dick is already hard and insistent, pressed against her heat. There are at least two layers of sweats separating us, but I can feel her through all of it.

"Beau," she breathes. My hand slides up her ribs until I can cup her breast. My teeth nip at her lips in a promise of what's to come.

We still have on too many clothes though. I make quick work of hers, pulling her shirt over her head and her sweats down her legs. Had I known she wasn't wearing anything underneath either, we would have been here long ago.

"Where's your panties, dirty girl?" I don't know where the words come from. I wasn't lying when I said I saved it all for her. I just didn't realize that's what I was doing all these years.

Sitting up on my knees, I look down at her glorious body. "How dirty are you? Should we find out?" Pulling her up, I reverse our positions. She looks lost.

"Take off my shirt," I say with a sigh. She scrambles to pull it over my head. "Now the pants." I do have on under-wear, so she pulls them both down with one tug. Her lustful gaze meets mine when she's done. "You know what you want. Take it." Her eyes grow wide before they slide down my body.

"I'm not good at this," she whispers.

"Hey," I say, pushing myself up on my elbows. "Look at me." Her gaze slowly meets mine again. "Do you see how hard you made me just playing cards? There's no standard you have to live up to. Just your touch will drive me crazy."

She smiles, then her head lowers. Her tongue takes a tentative lick, and I almost lose my mind. My growl must encourage her because her lips wrap around me.

Her mouth is warm, her tongue teasing as she slides down. The next time she bobs her head, I feel her throat. My hips rock before I can stop them.

I'm still on my elbows so I don't miss when one of her small hands wraps around me and the other finds her clit.

She plays with my tip as her hand pumps my shaft in a steady rhythm. It matches the pace she strokes herself with.

"Jesus," I swear. "You're going to make me come, and you haven't earned it yet."

"Earned?" she asks as her sweet lips pop off my dick.

"You heard me." I expect her to put up a fight, but she only stares at me. Honestly, I'm just winging it now. The only thing I know is I don't want to finish in her mouth. Not this time anyway. That can come later when my legs give out. Moving to my knees, I hold out a hand. "Come here."

She takes my hand, trusting me to take care of her. When she's flush against me, I place her hands on my shoulders, grasp her ass, and pull her up my thighs. I press inside her as she wrestles to hold on to me. She can't reach the bed with her knees. I'm in total control. I stare into her eyes as I start to press up using my thighs.

"Beau," she moans. Her eyes widen when I thrust again, then they relax. She presses her lips against mine.

I'm lost. I know I'm falling hard, but I have no idea how to keep her. So, I do what I can to burn the memory of me in her mind. I set a punishing pace. Her breath begins to come in panting, little gasps as she rubs against my body.

"I'm—I'm," she pants. I stop.

"Not until I say so," I growl. Her eyes pop open, and she sears me with a glare. She wiggles trying to get purchase on the bed, but she's still suspended on me. Her hands struggle to press her up hoping to find the rhythm again, but I won't let her. My body is flush to hers giving her no ability to finish. Finally, she gives up and settles against me.

That's when I begin building her orgasm again. It comes quicker this time, but I still deny what she wants. She doesn't give me warning this time though—she's getting smarter. I stop anyway even though we're both in pain now. I can't get off until she does. The third time we begin, she watches me out of one eye.

"Oh my god, Beau," she complains when we stop again. "I've heard of this, but I swear if you stop again I'm going to axe murder you." I slap her right ass cheek. Her eyes glaze over with lust.

"Be good," I hiss.

"Please, daddy. Make me come." It's my turn to be shocked. She's turned this whole game up a notch. It works because she gets what she wants as I thrust back up on my knees. It only takes twice more before her back arches. "Fuck," she screams and sinks her teeth into my shoulder.

"Harmony," I moan before my mind floats away. She's draped on my shoulder when my head clears again. I want to ask if she's okay, but I have to catch my breath first.

My thighs are screaming, my head is spinning, and I could really use something to drink, but I stay perfectly still holding her. I'm not done, not by a long shot. This is nice though, just sitting here.

"Can you help me down?" she finally asks.

"Hold on." I slowly bend forward until she's flat on her back. "Are you okay?"

"Yeah," she says with a grin. "That was crazy."

"Crazy good?"

"Crazy amazing." Her eyebrows knit. "Did I bite you?"

"I think so."

"I'm sorry."

"Why? I'm not." I try to see the mark on my shoulder, but it's just out of range. "Fucking sexy." I move so she can sit up. Her fingers graze the bite making me shiver.

"I don't think I broke the skin. You're going to have a

heck of a mark though," she says. "I'll be back, need to use the facilities."

"Do you want something to drink?" Hunting around, I finally find my sweats and step into them. Harmony, however, gathers up her clothes and walks naked to the bathroom. I take a moment to appreciate the red mark I left on her fabulous ass.

"Water would be good," she calls from the bathroom. "Maybe something to snack on?"

"I've got you." Reacher gets up from his pillow next to fire to follow me into the kitchen. I pour some food into his bowl and grab a bag of Chex Mix from the pantry. Pulling two bottles of water out of the fridge, I head back to the living room. Harmony walks in a few minutes later.

"Get the cards," she snaps. It takes a while, but eventually we've located them all. She shuffles them and deals. Her eyebrows are creased in concentration as she studies her cards. I'm not sure what's got her on edge, but I'll just wait it out. She snatches up cards and discards like we're locked in a death match.

"Gin," she announces after five minutes. That might be the fastest hand I've played. She tosses her cards down and stares at me. One eye squints as she studies me. Jesus, what have I done now? "So, I want to know who taught you that?"

"Taught me what?"

"That," she says, twirling an arm around as if that explains everything. "The bronc cowgirl maneuver. The delayed gratification thing." I try to keep a straight face. I really do, but I laugh anyway. Bronc cowgirl maneuver?

"Where did you learn the 'daddy' thing?" I say, trying to turn the tables on her.

"Obviously, I read." She crosses her arms over her chest to wait me out.

"Honestly, I just made it up." She scowls not believing a word I'm saying. "Okay, I may have Googled some stuff once."

"Well," she answers, "we may need to see about getting you better internet if that's what you're going to do in your spare time." She gathers up the cards a little more slowly this time. "Do you have anything else in that arsenal?"

"I have a few ideas I'd like to try."

"Good answer. We don't need these then." She tosses the cards in the air. As they rain down around us, I tackle her to the bed. "You know, I don't think I miss having TV at all," she adds with a laugh.

"Good answer."

thirteen

BEAU

"MERRY CHRISTMAS!" jerks me out of the best dream involving Harmony. I try to ignore the outburst and settle back into my fantasy. Except something in my brain tells me that wasn't either of us, and as far as I know, Reacher hasn't learned to converse in English. Yet.

"Wow, it looks like there was a hell of a frat party in here last night." That isn't one of us either. I pry one eye open to search the living room. There's a bigger, younger version of myself standing over me. "Why is there an eight of hearts stuck to your brother's forehead?" Fucking playing cards. I slap the one on my forehead away.

"Smells kind of like a frat party too," Travis says.

"Y'all shut up before you wake her," I growl, climbing from the makeshift bed.

"Speaking of...?"

I scowl at my little brother as I head for the bathroom. Closing the door, I look at myself in the mirror. My face sports the start of a mountain man beard and mustache.

It's gone from a shadow to something more in the last few days. It'll have to wait until there's hot water again. The idea of cold-water shaving makes me shudder.

My hair looks about as bad. Fortunately, I keep it short, so it just sticks up in strange directions. I turn the water on and try my best to convince it to lie down. A quick body wash, fresh deodorant, and I return to the living room. Harmony is still sound asleep. My brother and his boyfriend are at the kitchen table sipping coffee when I find them.

"How long has the electricity been out?" Travis asks.

"Day before yesterday?" Honestly, I can't remember. My mind is still muddled from lack of sleep. "How are y'all here anyway?"

"Trace has a buddy who owns a business that deals in armored cars and stuff. He lent us a tank."

"A tank?" This I have to see. Walking back in the living room, I sweep the edge of the curtain back. Sitting in front of the house is something that does look like a tank. At the very least, something the military would use. Huh. That would be a good thing to have, but based on the emblem on the front, it was out of my price range.

"So, I guess you and Harmony are getting along?" Travis asks when I return to the kitchen. I shrug. "She's a really nice person, you know." My gaze meets his. "Sorry, she got stranded with you. If I'd known, well—"

"Well what?" I challenge. Was my little brother trying to warn me off. It's too late if he is, but I'm not going to tell him that. As a matter of fact, it's none of his business what goes on between us.

"Nothing," he mumbles.

"The electricity went out," I bark. "It's freezing in the bedrooms, so the pull-out couch was the next best thing.

What did you want me to do, huh, Travis? What are you trying to say?" I glare at him.

"I don't think he's saying anything, it's just—" Trace started.

"Hi," Harmony says from the doorway. She's wrapped one of the blankets around her. "Merry Christmas," she adds.

We all turn to look at her. Travis jumps up to pull her into a hug. She laughs before pushing him back.

"I must smell awful. We've been without hot water for ages. Let me go see what I can do in the bathroom. Oh, I let Reacher out," she says to me as she walks to the bathroom.

"She's even more gorgeous in person," Trace points out.

"Right?" Travis agrees. He tilts his head at me when a growl slips up from my chest.

"Did you have breakfast?" I ask. I stand and move to the pantry trying to divert my attention away from my brother and his boyfriend's conjecture of what Harmony and I have been up to.

They could also take a break from pointing out how beautiful she is. Not that I'm territorial or anything. Yeah, I know. If I can't handle that, how would I ever handle the crowds who all want a piece of her on tour?

"Oh, we brought so much food," Trace announces, jumping up. "It's all in these amazing coolers in the back of the truck. We weren't sure how much food you'd have, so we brought Christmas dinner. Come help me bring it in, Trav." He takes Travis's hand and pulls him up from the chair. "We even brought breakfast."

"Where did they go?" Harmony asks, stepping back into the kitchen. I hand her a cup of coffee fixed just the way she likes it—very little coffee, a lot of cream and sugar.

"I think they brought half of Austin with them." Taking

her free hand, I lead her to the living room window. Outside, Travis and Trace are loading their arms with containers of food. Harmony rushes over to open the door when they head in with their first load.

"There's more," Travis announces happily. We watch as they return outside for another load.

If I was nice, I'd help. I'm not that nice. I also believe that by the time I got my boots on, they'd have it unloaded. Besides, I'll have to go outside this evening to feed the horses. One trip into the arctic weather seems like enough.

"Presents!" Travis says, walking back inside. He stops at the tree and unloads his arms. "Hey, nice tree. It's been ages since you've had one of these." He steps back and appraises it. "This was your doing, wasn't it?" He turns to look at Harmony.

"Beau helped," she answers. His eyebrows raise high enough to hit the ceiling.

"What?" I snarl.

"Please tell me you made him cut out the snowflakes."

"He did! The good ones are his. He also helped with the garland. And he chopped it down." She beams over at me making my heart miss a beat. "We even rode to the neighbors to borrow lights. I wish you could see them, they're so pretty."

Travis looks over at me with his mouth opened dramatically in shock. I roll my eyes, but it doesn't feel so bad having her brag on me.

None of it really took much effort. It was all worth it though seeing how happy it makes her. It makes me wish I had made more effort for my brother over the last couple of years. Even grown, he deserves more from me.

"Well, I think you both did an outstanding job," Trace adds from the kitchen doorway.

"Thank you, Trace. At least someone is appreciative," I say.

"I'm appreciative," Travis argues. "Just totally shocked is all."

"Speaking of shocked," Trace continues. "Is the ham in the fridge for dinner? We brought a turkey, sides and dessert."

"Yeah, I bought a smoked one before the snowstorm since y'all were coming this year."

"Mind if I start working on it?"

"Knock yourself out." Did I mention my brother had the good sense to date a chef from one of Austin's most popular restaurants. The man can cook rings around anyone I've ever met. He'll take that ham and turn it into something worthy of a Michelin star.

"Can I help?" Harmony asks.

"Absolutely, and I'll bring a lovely piece of German stollen out to the both of you in a moment. Come, love." I watch as they disappear into the kitchen. Travis moves to the couch and begins folding it up. Reacher wanders in while we wrestle with sliding the cushions back into place. We're presented with breakfast and top offs of our coffee as soon as we sit down.

"How are you doing?" Travis asks the minute they return to the kitchen. "Like, really?" He turns toward me pulling his leg onto his opposite knee.

"Travis," I warn.

"I know, I know. Don't ask too many questions about Beau's private life. Don't act like I worry about him way out here. Don't question his life choices. What am I missing?" he says with a dismissive wave of his hand. "You know what sucks about that? I have to be an open book. You're the only one that gets to hide away."

"I don't hide away."

"Really? Then what's happening between you and Harmony because something is."

Damn my little brother and his astute powers of observation.

"It's none of your business. Just like you and Trace are none of mine. It doesn't matter anyway, she's leaving. We'd never work out. End of story."

"Fine," he pouts. "Just eat your weird glazed fruit bread I had to help make, and we'll sit here in silence. Like normal."

I take a slow drawn-out bite of stollen while glaring at Travis. He tries to stay irritated with me, but it never lasts long. It's part of why he's the only brother I've ever wanted. Because, inside, he really is the best man I know. It scares me to think he can't say the same about me.

"So, what did you get me for Christmas?" His 100-watt smile lights up his face.

"You're as bad as Harmony. She spent all day before Christmas Eve harassing me about her presents."

"How did you manage to buy her a present? Trace and I brought her several, but we could still get to the shops."

"Who says I bought them?"

"Did you draw her something?" He's way too excited about this. "She's going to be so stoked. She's getting a M. Rayburn original." I roll my eyes at him. It seems I'm doing that a lot today.

"It's not a big deal," I say.

"It is a big deal," he answers. "Dude, the gallery said people are starting to ask for them. They keep raising the prices."

I shrug. I know my royalty checks keep getting larger, but I hadn't questioned why. I should be cutting Travis in.

He was the one who made the arrangements with the gallery.

I never intended to sell any of my sketches. I never thought they were good enough. I guess that's something Harmony and I have in common. We both have Travis to thank for our rising fame.

"Do you know that Trace and I have already met?" Harmony announces, bursting back into the room. Trace follows on her heels carrying a fancy looking coffee pot. "It's true." She plops down on the couch against me. Travis's stupid eyebrows hit the roof again.

"I didn't realize he is the chef at Jon Caprese's Steakhouse in Austin. I ate there not long ago. So good," she says, looking at Trace who's now beaming at her from the lounge chair. "You came out and asked if I liked the steak."

"And you said it was one of the best you'd ever had," Trace says. "You even said we were one of your go-tos on that morning show interview."

"I wasn't lying. Beau," she says, grabbing my hand, "you have to try the filet mignon. To. Die. For."

"I have," I answer. "It is."

"I can't believe I'm eating Christmas dinner designed by Chef Trace." He blushes over her gushing. I wasn't lying, the man can fucking cook. "So, tell me everything about you two. How did you meet?" It's Travis who blushes this time.

"I had a class on tort law. We had to pick an industry that sees a lot of cases, so I chose the restaurant industry. I have a friend who knows the manager at Jon's. The day I had scheduled to interview him, he came down with a nasty run of flu. Trace offered to step in. A quick meeting turned into hours, which turned into dinner, and the rest is history as they say."

"I walked out of the kitchen, took one look at this guy,

and was smitten," Trace says, reaching for my brother's hand. They grin at each other for a minute.

"Awww," Harmony coos. "Such a great meet cute."

"What's a meet cute?" I ask. It's like she talks in code half the time.

"It's a cute story of how someone meets. Ours would be snowed in, forced proximity," she answers. I swear to God, if Travis doesn't learn to control his damn eyebrows, I'm going to shave them off. "Well, forced isn't the right word."

"I'd call it a little brother's best friend, close proximity," Trace says.

"Yeah, that sounds better," she agrees.

"Hold on, I think this is more just one friend taking care of another," I argue. My definition sucks. Not winning any awards for my storyline.

"Ooh, friends-to-lovers," Trace points out.

"Strangers-to-lovers?" Travis tries out. "But I think best friend's older brother is better."

"Okay," I say, trying to end this conversation. Jesus, people are exhausting.

fourteen

HARMONY

IS it wrong to gang up with your friend and his boyfriend to pick on his brother? Beau has a tell when something is stressing him out. One eye squints. It's adorable. The more we talk about romantic tropes, the more squinty he's getting. Travis winks at me. He knows that tell also I assume.

"Oh, there's always the daddy/daughter one," Travis says.

"That's it," Beau announces as he pushes off the couch. "I'm going out to move more firewood. Reacher!" The dog reluctantly gets off his pillow to follow. Somehow, we all manage to keep it in until we hear the mudroom door slam, then we burst out laughing.

"I always knew you were the best," Travis says through his laughter. "I've got to be honest. I wouldn't mind having you as a sister-in-law." Well, that sobers me up in a hurry. Sister-in-law?

"Travis, you didn't strand me here on purpose did you, like some twisted *Beauty and the Beast* thing?"

"No," he says, placing his palm over his heart. "I promise that was not my intention. But I have to admit it was a good happenstance."

"I agree," chimes in Trace. "I haven't seen Beau this festive ever. He's even more relaxed than normal."

"If this is relaxed, I'd hate to see him uptight." Although, I'm pretty sure that was the Beau I found at the stove the first morning I was here. I have to agree, he's much better now.

"Seriously though, of everyone I know, you're the only one who's managed to make him chill a little." Travis shakes his head. "After Mom and Dad died, he took on so much. Way more than any teenager should. I think he got so used to always having to be ahead of the game, he just stopped living for himself."

"That had to be so hard on both of you," Trace says, taking his hand again.

"It was. Except I had Beau to fall on. Who did he have? Not eight-year-old me, that's for sure." We sit in silence as the question echoes around the room.

I wish I had been Beau's age when it happened. Maybe I could have been the person he turned to when he was hurting. But I was way too young to know anything much about grief that profound.

"Well, anyway, let's not let it mess up Christmas," Travis says. "What are the plans for the day?"

"Dinner should be ready between one and two," Trace answers.

"We can open presents after that," I add.

"Until then, I know Trace brought everything to make gingerbread men and sugar cookies."

"I did that." Trace stands and drags us both to our feet. Before I know it, we're happily cutting cookies out of dough with Christmas cutters that Trace also brought. I've just added a star to the cookie sheet when Beau blows back in looking frozen.

"Damn, it's still colder than a witches—" He stops when he sees me wrist deep in cookie dough. "Is that sugar cookies?"

"It is," I say. "Here." Peeling a piece of dough off, I hold it toward him. His gaze turns stormy as he sucks it from my fingers with his lips.

"Whew," Trace exclaims, fanning his face. "Is it getting hot in here, or is it just me?"

"It's mostly you, sweetie. But, that was pretty good too," Travis answers. "You know what we need? Music. Do you still have all of the Ed Sheeran albums, Beau?"

"Ed Sheeran, huh? I approve," I tease.

"I do, but how do you propose we play them? There's no electricity remember."

"Oh, I've got this. I brought a guitar," Travis says. "Wash up and make cookies. Maybe we can convince a certain someone to play us a tune while we're at it."

He jogs into the living room, and we hear the front door open. He returns a few minutes later with an acoustic guitar. Pulling it from the case, I strum a few chords. Not bad. Then I start singing my favorite Ed Sheeran. I know every song on my favorite playlist by heart. I've got this.

They hoot and holler every time I begin a new song. Beau watches me so intently I wonder if he even realizes he's made close to ten donkeys out of sugar cookie dough.

Travis and Trace take turns dancing around the kitchen and working on cookies. I haven't had this much fun performing since that night on the picnic table. I wish they could tour with me all the time.

I continued to sing until it was time to set the table for Christmas dinner. Beau and I pulled the table out from the wall while the others worked on the food. Beau disappeared for a moment and reappeared with a beautiful Christmas tablecloth. It was white with hand embroidered holly running along the edges.

"Hey, you kept Mom's favorite tablecloth." Travis grins at Beau. "She did the handwork on it," he adds to me. "She was always sewing stuff. Did you keep her dishes too?"

"Of course." Beau motions to me to follow him toward the back of the house. When we get to his bedroom, he closes the door and pulls me to him. "The dishes are in one of the closets, but I really just wanted you alone for half a second." He bends and kisses me. "Jesus, you taste like sugar cookie," he whispers when he stands back up.

"Are you sure? Maybe you should check again." This time, he doesn't just kiss me, he picks me up and presses me against the wall of his bedroom. I wrap my legs around his waist as he trails kisses down my jaw, to my neck, and over my shoulder.

"Hey, guys," Travis yells from the kitchen. "We really need the table set before the food gets cold." Beau gives me a frustrated smirk when he stands back up straight. Slowly, he eases me to my feet.

"There's something to be said for a quiet Christmas you know," he says with a scowl.

"You don't mean that. You love having your brother and Trace here," I scold back. He opens a small closet door and starts filling my arms with dishes from one of the shelves. "These are wonderful." The plates have Christmas trees on them.

"Mom inherited them from an aunt. She always loved them. I figured I'd hang onto them for Travis." We carry them back down the hallway to the kitchen.

After laying all of the dishes and silverware out, I return to the closet for an assortment of candlesticks and candles. The fact that I have to find them using a lantern isn't lost on me. It's ridiculous. But at least the table looks nice.

"Food is coming in hot. Reacher, go lay down," Travis says, setting the first dish on the table. Beau and I move out of the way as he and Trace move everything to the table.

I'm not sure how they produced so much food without electricity. I think there is more than I've ever seen before. Everything from a glazed ham to sweet potato casserole cover from one end of the table to the other.

"This looks amazing," I say as Trace adds a basket of rolls. "I can already tell I'm going to eat way too much. My moaning later will be on your head."

"Not Beau's?" He smirks back. My face instantly catches fire. Blushing sucks. You can't even deny anything when your face gives you away.

"Busted," Travis says with a laugh. I sneak a glimpse of Beau. There's a scowl on his face, but it's just as red as mine. Yeah, we've been busted. I wait for Beau to start a rampage against his brother. Instead, he shrugs and picks up a piece of ham. "Really, nothing?"

"What do you want me to say?"

"This is just so not you. And it's your turn to say grace. Put that ham down." Beau sets his fork on his plate and takes my hand. I would think this is a wild declaration of us as a couple except he takes Trace's hand across from him. Apparently, it's a hand holding family.

His prayer is short, but gets the job done without being showy. I appreciate that. My father always went on way too long. It was like he was trying to get in every event for the last year in one rambling head-bowed speech. I'm not sure I've ever eaten a hot Thanksgiving dinner before.

"What's the rest of your tour look like?" Trace asks me. Wow, this is the last thing I want to think about right now. But I would never say that. There's nothing worse than someone who bitches about the amazing opportunities she's been given.

"Tucson is next, then there are a couple in California. I have a small break, then it's off to Charleston. I don't remember after that. My label has me ping-ponging around for a while. I won't see my place for a long time it seems," I answer.

"When do you get time off?" Trace asks.

"Summer maybe?" I don't really know. I'm still small potatoes in the music world. I go where and when they tell me. Don't get me wrong. I love what I do. I just wish it wasn't so much sometimes. "I'll have a couple of weeks, then it's into the studio."

I'm actually excited to go to work on the next album. That tune I keep humming has been forming words in my mind. I can't wait to put it down.

"That sounds exhausting," Travis says.

"No more than law school, I imagine."

"At least I don't have to live out of a suitcase."

"It's not so bad. There are some musicians that thrive on it. They actually finish their tours in better shape than they were in when they started."

"Like Beau. Can you image how old and fat he would get if he left here." Travis grins when Beau throws his hands up in consternation. "Big ole beer gut."

"He'd still be a stunner. A real man bear," I point out.

"See," Beau says, pointing his knife at his brother. "I'm not worried. I'll just become a silver fox man bear."

"Keep dreaming," Travis says.

"I don't know. A little gray at the temples. Maybe a sexy graying beard. You'd better watch out, I might start checking out the older brother," Trace answers.

"You keep dreaming. I'm the only man you'll ever want."

"True." Trace leans over to give Travis a quick peck on the cheek. Why are cheek kisses so sweet? It makes me want to swoon. They're almost as good as the forehead kisses Beau doles out. "Now, who's ready for dessert?"

"Oh god," I moan. Travis and Trace exchange a grin. I swear I'm saying nothing from now on. It's like dealing with a group of teenage boys.

"How about we clean up while y'all chill in the living room?" Beau suggests. "You cooked. Harmony and I can take care of this."

"Yeah, you can, dog." Travis laughs as he gets up from the table.

"Jesus," Beau breathes. They're still laughing when they reach the living room. Beau pushes up from the table. "They're like having two obnoxious brothers. I don't remember him being this bad in high school."

"Did you have a lot of women over when he was in high school?" I ask, helping him stack plates on the counter by the sink.

"Never. It didn't seem like a good role model to have a revolving door of women at the house." He fills the kettle and sets it on the stove to heat.

"Exactly. This is new, and he can't help teasing you about it. He's just having some fun."

"I know, but thanks for not trying to flee out the door." I

lean against the counter while we wait for the water to heat. "He doesn't really bother me though. You do. I'm desperate to throw you over my shoulder and haul you to my bedroom."

He fists my hair and pulls me against him. His lips brush against mine tentatively before crushing them in a brutal kiss. His tongue insists on controlling mine as if he's desperately trying to imprint his touch in my mind.

He doesn't have to worry. I couldn't forget him if I tried. The kettle whistles, and he pulls back. His hand stays in my hair for a few more moments as he traces my face with his dark gaze.

Then he's gone, and I hate that stupid kettle with my whole being. How will I survive on the road knowing he's so far away? I don't even want to be in the next room without him there. Is this what love feels like? Leaving is going to be harder than I expected.

"Do you want me to put more water on for tea? Or do you want hot chocolate?" he asks. Is he feeling what I am, or is he able to chalk this up to nothing more than a chance encounter? He sets the kettle on without waiting for my answer. I grab a dish towel and move next to him. Silently, we wash and dry the dishes.

"I know I don't have any right to say this," he says quietly. "This is gutting me. I'm not ready for you to go."

"Me too." He nods his head without looking at me. I help him haul the dishes back to the closet and put them away.

It won't do any good to ruin the day by trying to reason out how to be together. His life is here, mine is somewhere else. So, we do the only thing left to us. We carry heaping mugs of hot chocolate and plates of pie into the living room.

fifteen

BEAU

I KNOW nothing can come from it, but I had to say the words. I'm not ready to let her go. There's just no way I can make our worlds work together. I guess I needed her to know how I felt. I don't really know.

I don't know anything anymore. What am I trying to do, but make us both miserable? I really hope someday she looks back on this Christmas with a smile. She'll tell her kids that this was one of the best she ever had.

"Dessert!" she announces with a flourish as we walk into the living room.

"Perfect. We were starting to waste away in here," Travis teases. I think it's more likely he'll reach man bear status faster than I will. Especially constantly eating Trace's cooking. "I have a question. I know the super artsy snowflakes are Beau's, but how in the heck did you cut a nativity scene into that one?"

"It's not hard." It wasn't, you just have to know how to

fold the paper. Also, you have to visualize the area to cut out. "Okay, maybe there's more to it than normal."

"Easy for you to say. You got all of Mom's art genes. And Dad's brainiac genes. Also, all the athletic ability from Uncle Kyle."

"And you got all of the whiny ones from whatever dog we owned at the time apparently." My brother has always been under the impression that I'm the more gifted brother. He forgets how brilliant he is in front of a crowd. He will work his way to the Supreme Court one day, I have no doubt.

"But, Beau," he whines, stretching my name into an impossible number of syllables. I respond by rolling my eyes when he grins at me. "Hey, when do we get to open presents?"

"Now, please," Harmony pleads.

"Why do I have to decide?" I ask.

"Because you're the only voice of reason in this house," Trace answers. "But, yeah, I vote presents."

"Then open presents," I snap. "Jesus."

I think I growled hard enough even the electricity was intimidated because it chose that moment to come back on. We all freeze as the Christmas tree sparkles back to life. The heater fires up, and one of the living room lights glows in the corner.

"Hold on." I jump up to turn the generator off and check that all of the pilot lights reignited. When I return, Harmony has Trace and Travis posed in front of the tree while she snaps a photo.

"Your turn," Trace says, pointing to me. I step behind Harmony and wrap my arms around her for a photo. He's been taking them the whole day, but this is the first chance we've had to get the tree in all its glory. "Now presents," he adds when we sit back down. "Hold on, how come nobody noticed the stockings?"

He grabs four from the mantle. I didn't get a ton for them, but each one has candy and a few things for each person. Reacher has his own filled with toys and treats. He barks as Travis offers him a bone out of it. I watch as everyone digs through their stockings. Harmony's might be my favorite.

"Whose signature is this?" she asks, pulling an old guitar pick out.

"Wait, is that the one that Dad had?" Travis asks. "The one with Billy Gibbons's initials. That's brilliant!"

"Oh my gosh," Harmony says in awe. "I can't keep this."

"You absolutely can. Dad would have loved it going to you. He loved music," Travis adds. "Nice job, Beau." I shrug. It was Santa after all.

"This is the best thing I've ever gotten." Her gaze catches mine. She's hugging the pick. Her face lights up when I smile.

"Dude," Travis says, pulling out a tie pin with Dad's initials on it. The cufflinks farther down in his stocking match it.

"What is it?" Trace asks.

"These were Dad's."

"A lawyer needs a good set of cuff links and a tie pin," I answer. I've held on to them forever waiting for him to be old enough to appreciate them.

"Shut up, asshole. You're going to make me cry," Travis sniffs.

"I love these," Trace says, holding up a set of silver measuring spoons in the shape of bluebonnets. I found them in a small shop last time I was in Austin. Trace collects odd measuring spoons. I don't understand it, but to each his own. "And so as not to be outdone." He pulls my stocking out from behind the tree and presents it to me.

"Yeah, thought we wouldn't think of it, didn't you?" Travis asks.

"Well, you didn't," Trace points out.

Inside the stocking I find a gift card to an online bookstore. It's so much easier to buy books for my reader than try to get to a bookstore or the library. Books are one of my must-have items. I just budget for them every month like most people do utility bills. There are also chocolates from a specialty shop and several other fun things.

"Thanks, guys."

"No, it was Santa," Travis reminds me. "When we were little, Mom had a rule that if you stop believing in Santa Claus, then he stops coming. I don't think either one of us will admit to this day that he's not real."

"I love that," Harmony says. "Your mom was a genius."

"Don't even get us started on the Easter bunny. Who wants to go first?"

"Let me," Trace answers. He moves to the tree and fishes out a handful of presents. After handing them out, he waits anxiously as we unwrap everything.

"Music paper!" Harmony exclaims, opening hers.

"I figured you probably write on a computer, but thought it would be fun for you to put a song on it and frame it," he explains. "Or give it to your favorite chef, signed, to put up in his restaurant office."

"Thank you. That's exactly what I'm going to do."

The rest of us open our presents. I get a new sketch pad and set of pencils. Perfect timing since mine are down to the nubs. Travis gets an official looking briefcase with his initials on it. He spends forever opening every pocket inside and testing the locks.

Trace bought Harmony a silver cuff for her arm. She gushes over it until Travis jumps up.

"My turn," he announces. He passes out his gifts, and we take turns opening them. Travis always buys me clothes for Christmas. I think he doesn't believe I'm capable of clothing myself. I've explained to him a thousand times there is nothing wrong with buying your clothes at the farm store. I hold up my colorful angora sweater for Harmony to appreciate. She grins.

"Oh, Travis. This is beautiful," she says, holding up hers in complementary colors. Is he setting us up for a catalog model-worthy date night? We'd look like something from a Hallmark movie. I'll keep it, though, and bring it out when I visit him.

"Do you want to go next, bro?" Travis asks.

"Sure." Standing, I wander over to the tree. Since I'm usually a crap brother the rest of the year, I try to splurge a little at Christmas. I bought Trace a couple of pieces from the knife set he's been drooling over. Not the entire set— that would cost me the equivalent of a mortgage. Who knew knives could be so expensive.

Travis always claims just paying his living expenses while he works to finish school is enough present for him. I don't agree. I bought him a set of high-end headphones for when he's studying and a new laptop to replace the one I got him when he left for undergrad. He squeals and hugs it to him. I mean, that other laptop is getting pretty banged up.

"I made you something. Don't expect much," I tell Harmony, giving her a rolled-up tube. It's the sketch I did of her. She opens it slowly and stares at it. I thought it was pretty good, but her reaction makes me nervous. I'm sure she gets this kind of thing all the time from her fans. It was stupid of me to think she'd want another one.

"It's amazing," she whispers. "You drew this?" Her blue gaze glances up at me. I shrug. Slowly, she stands and hands Travis the drawing. She throws her arms around my waist in a fierce hug. "It's the best thing I've ever gotten." Her lips meet mine in a searing kiss.

"Hey, I didn't get that kind of thank you," Travis mock whines at us.

"You missed your chance in high school," she teases, stepping back.

"Dumbass," I add without breaking eye contact with her. She grins back.

"But then, you wouldn't have Trace in your life."

"True," Travis agrees.

"And I'm starting to think I like the older brother a little better."

"Fair."

"Besides, it's my turn now," she says, turning to the tree. Somehow, she manages to do a happy hop thing to it. All she needs is an elf outfit to complete the look. My mind turns for a moment to Harmony in a sexy, filthy elf suit. I don't even try anymore to keep the thoughts at bay. I think they'll be the only thing left to occupy me at night soon.

"Okay, I don't have anything yet for you guys. But I thought you might enjoy a weekend in Nashville when I get back. I can take you to tour the studio and meet a few A-listers," she says.

"That sounds great," Trace says as he looks at a grinning Travis. "We can definitely carve out some time to do that."

"That will be so much fun." She pulls out a wrapped package from under the tree and lays it in my lap. "I made you something totally not as amazing as your drawing, but I hope you'll use them until I can get the real thing."

She watches anxiously as I pull the paper from a small box. Inside is an array of homemade frames. "I thought you could add more photos to the wall in your office. Maybe of you and Travis as adults."

"That's a great idea," Travis says.

I slowly pick through the frames looking at each one as I lay it on the table. She's used the supplies I found in the office to make them. One has a picture of us at Travis's high school graduation. Another is obviously meant for a photo of Reacher. I hold it up for him to see, but he ignores me choosing to focus on the bone in front of him instead.

"Thank you," I say, looking up at her worried face. "You're not replacing them." There's no way I'm letting her trade for a bunch of soulless metal frames bought at a store. Each one of these says something about her and how she sees me. There's even one with cowboy stickers she must have dug out of somewhere.

"I know it's not much, but—"

"I love them." Taking her hand, I pull her down until she's straddling my thighs. "I love them," I whisper, pulling her to me. I kiss her gently on the lips.

"You never mentioned, Travis, that your Christmas festivities were X-rated," Trace teases. I don't care if they're uncomfortable. This will all end soon, and I'm not passing up any opportunity to kiss Harmony before she leaves.

"They used to be very Hallmark," Travis answers. "I'm not sure what happened. These are more interesting though." Harmony shifts off my lap, and I let her go. If I didn't have my little brother and his boyfriend sitting in the same room, I'd never let her go. "Speaking of, we need to think about heading out of this winter wonderland. We need to make miles while it's still daylight."

I stand mechanically from the couch. Harmony leaves to pack her bag. I help pack up the presents, including an extra I slip in with Harmony's box. Trace helps me clean up while Travis hauls everything to their truck.

I can't think of a thing that can prevent the inevitable from happening. She's about to sweep out of my life just like she swept in. Fate is just too much of a bitch to care.

"Ready, sweetheart?" Travis asks as Harmony wheels her suitcase out of the back room.

"I think so." I follow them out of the house. Travis takes her suitcase to the truck while we say goodbye. I don't know what to say. I guess Harmony doesn't really either. She raises on her toes, presses a soft kiss to my lips, and walks down the steps. She doesn't look back as she crawls into the back seat of the vehicle.

I offer one last wave as they pull out from the front of the house. In a few minutes, they're down the road. Just like that, our time is over. I don't want to go back in the house. It'll feel too empty without her in it. Reacher must feel the same as he presses against me. His mournful gaze meets mine.

"I know, boy," I say, patting his head. "I already miss her too."

sixteen

HARMONY

THE WORST THING you can do when your heart is breaking is to turn around and look over your shoulder. That's exactly what I do. Well, not quite, it was more like a face pressed against the window experience. Same thing, though.

The last thing I see is Beau standing on the porch, his jeans tucked into his boots and a stocking cap pulled over his messy hair. Reacher sits pressed against his leg.

Neither Travis nor Trace even try to say any words of comfort. I wouldn't have listened anyway. My heart is waging a war inside.

Everything inside me wants to turn right back around, but I know I have obligations that take me away. How can somewhere you've only known a few short days already feel like home? I'm already homesick, and we've barely cleared the gate.

"Are we passing the Dairy Queen on the way?" I ask.

"Yeah, why?" Travis answers.

"Because I could use the biggest ass dipped cone they can make." That's one of the best things about being back in Texas. The ice cream places never close. You can still get an ice cream cone with a foot of snow on the ground. Except it's Christmas and even Dairy Queen isn't open on Christmas.

I slump in my seat and try to run through everything I need to do when I get to Austin. My assistant will need to be on the top of that list. She'll book me a flight to catch up with the tour.

Then, I guess I should call my family and let them know I'm alive. I'm not sure they'll have noticed that I've been out of touch. They might be further down the list.

We finally pass into cell phone range, and mine goes nuts. Notifications light it up like there's no tomorrow.

I should be grateful that Travis let me charge it in the truck as we lumber along. I'm not really. It was nice to be so far off the grid for a little while. I scroll through the messages hoping, in the back of my mind, that there's one from Beau. There's not.

Robin, however, has left enough for a novel. There are also enough voicemails to fill up the phone and emails stacked on top of emails. Gross.

Beau and I never discussed if we would stay in touch. I've heard the best thing would be just to move on. I should go cold turkey, no contact whatsoever. I don't know if I'm that strong.

"So," Travis finally says. "Are you okay?"

"Yeah, great. No problems here. Just peachy. Can't wait to get back on the road. Yep, just call me living the dream," I answer.

They share a look I understand immediately. It says, she might be losing it. They might be right. "Shit," I groan.

"Why didn't you warn me it was so easy to fall for your brother?"

"Then, you did fall for him?"

"Yes." I'm so miserable. They give me a reprieve by staying silent for much of the drive. Eventually, we pull up to the hotel I stayed at last time. "Thanks, Travis. Please come see me guys. I'd love that."

"Harmony," Travis says, turning around in his seat. Trace gets out to help me with my bag. It's probably an attempt to give us a little privacy. "Whatever happens from here, you know you can always go home, right?"

I don't really understand what he's talking about. Nashville is my home now. "Home will be right where you left him," he adds. Oh. I squeeze his arm and open my door.

Giving Trace one last hug, I take my bag from him and wheel it through the hotel door.

Travis makes everything seem so easy, but he's wrong. Life is never that simple. There is always something keeping you away from the thing that will make you happiest. It's best just to smile and press forward. I'm sure Beau will soon be just a sweet distant memory.

I check in and call Robin on my way to my room. My mind is soon whirling with schedules, appearances, studio time, and a myriad of other things. I hang up with her and take a long, hot shower.

Room service delivers dinner that I eat in one of the fuzzy robes before falling into a bed that feels like a cloud. None of it makes me smile. I fall to sleep dreaming about Beau snuggled up against me on that lumpy, old pull-out couch.

The next morning, I'm woken bright and early by banging on my door. Hair and makeup are standing outside when I open it. Heaven forbid me catching a flight to Arizona not looking perfectly coifed.

My wardrobe arrives next. It's a white jumpsuit studded with rhinestones. The boots are the best part—they have fringe!

My flight is a rush of TSA, lounges, and early boarding. I try to smile and wave when someone recognizes me. Being recognized is still an odd feeling. All of this seems so surreal.

Every few minutes I check my phone just in case a certain someone sends me a text. He hasn't, and I haven't sent him one either. Maybe he's using my original radio silence idea.

"Harmony!" Robin greets me when I arrive in Arizona. "I am so glad you made it out of that nightmare safely." I open my mouth to argue, but I'm swept out of the airport and into the back of an SUV.

"We have so much to go over. We'll start first with your schedule for today." I tune her out as she goes over every minute of my day. I don't really need to listen. She'll make sure I get where I need to be.

The desert scenery slides by as I gaze out the window. Robin asks several times if I'm even paying attention. I profess that I am, even though that's the farthest thing from the truth.

My thoughts are focused several states away wondering what Beau and Reacher have planned for today. What are they doing at this very minute? Are they feeding the horses, feeding the cattle? Are they warm and safe?

Plastering a smile on my face, I step out of the car. Robin checks us into the hotel. They're all the same. I wonder if it would be different if Beau were here with me? I have to get over this and start focusing on my career again.

With a monumental effort, I pull my thoughts away from that ranch in Texas and back to tonight's performance.

"Hello, Tucson," I yell, stepping onto the stage hours later. We're in a theater at one of the colleges. The band starts into the first set, and I join in. I give it everything I have, but there's a piece of my heart not in this. I truly hope the fans can't tell. Nothing would be worse than giving them less than my all.

When we're done, I go through the same routine I do everywhere, and we head to the next concert.

Tomorrow will be another day, another place, and another chance to shine. It's fine. I'm fine. Everything is fine. Hopefully if I say it enough, it'll come true.

Lying in a bunk in the back of the bus, I roll over to check my phone. He's still not reached out.

"Hey, are you doing all right?" Robin asks from the next bunk. "It doesn't seem like your heart has been in this since before Christmas. What happened while you were snowed in?"

"Have you ever felt you were missing something in life?" I ask.

"No way. How could I? This is like living in a dream."

"Yeah," I agree. I roll over and close my eyes. She doesn't get it. I don't think anyone does.

I'm almost asleep when my phone pings. There are only a handful of people who can bypass my Do-Not-Disturb setting. My parents, my sister, Robin, and, very recently, Beau. I snatch the phone up praying it's none of the first three. I grin when I see the text.

. . .

Beau: I think I read where you're supposed to break things off cold turkey. It's a stupid plan. I can't do it anymore. I need to know how you are.

Me: I'm so glad you think that's stupid. I do too. I'm okay. How are you? How's Reacher?

Beau: The dog is still moping around looking for you. I might be too. Things are finally starting to melt. Lots of mud. Where are you now?

Me: Somewhere between Tucson and San Diego I think.

Beau: Too far.

I grin and set the phone down. We don't have to say anymore right now. Just knowing he's thinking about me is enough. Knowing he's missing me is everything.

I fall asleep and get the best rest I have since we've been apart. I wake the next morning with the same smile I fell asleep with.

"Someone woke up on the right side of the bed this morning," Robin says. The guys turn to look at me as I walk down the length of the bus. "Does it have something to do with the text you got last night?"

"Could be," I answer. "I just know I slept like a baby last night." I flop down in the dinette next to our drummer. "What's the agenda today?"

The band glances at each other with raised eyebrows. If they think this is a good mood, they should see me the morning after all-night sex with Beau. I snatch a doughnut from the box on the table and settle in to listen.

Every day is pretty much like the last. Robin has these meetings so were all on the same page. The days we perform are punctuated by sound checks, wardrobe changes, and performing like my life depends on it.

I guess, in a way, it does. I can't afford to have a bad performance no matter how I'm feeling. It would end my career before it even really gets going.

"When do we get back to Tennessee?" I ask, raising my hand like I'm in elementary school.

"We have a short break in February. Only a week, though, then we're right back out there," she answers.

I see a couple of the guys slump in their seats. I understand now. Luke has two small girls at home, and Chris and his wife are expecting their first in a couple of months. I'm sure Kip and Kenny miss home too. As for me, well, I'd like to see a little more of my hometown.

"We'll be back in Texas again in March, right?" Chris asks.

"Yes, then the south through April, then you're off until time to hit the studio. I'm thinking June at the earliest." Chris sighs in relief. I was very insistent when we made the schedule to have him home for the birth.

"I promise you'll be there, no matter what," I assure him. "I didn't spend all of my time hiding during Christmas either. I've almost finished a new song for the next album. If we can put a couple more together while we're driving, I think we won't need to spend a lot of time in studio."

"I'm game," Luke agrees. The rest of the guys nod.

"I'd like to debut this first one when we're in Texas next, if that's okay."

"That would be perfect," Robin says. "I'll make sure it gets leaked as a preview exclusive. They'll go wild."

She's talking about the social media influencers who follow my every step. I work really hard to keep on their good side. They're like paparazzi for today's world. "Will you for sure have it ready for Dallas?" she ask.

"If we can sneak in some extra rehearsal time."

"Consider it done." Robin hurries to the back of the bus to start working on the promo side of the release.

"Can we see it?" Kenny asks. He's the band's bass player. I can't write his part, but I have no doubt he'll have something amazing put together in no time.

"Yeah, let me grab it." I pull the song from my closet in the back of the bus and return to the table. I feel my anxiety amp up when I set the lyrics down. I grab my guitar and play the opening bars for them.

"Wow, Harmony. This is the best thing you've written. What happened during that week in Texas?" Kenny says. He slides the pages to Luke. They each take a turn looking at the song before the brainstorming starts.

I love this part of music. I might be the main vocalist, but we all have an equal stake in writing the music. It's why we're one of those rare country western groups instead of a solo artist or duet.

It takes hardly any time at all before we're practicing the new song in the very limited space we have. Now, I just hope he shows up to listen to it. It's about him, us really. It's the most personal thing I've ever written. It's about going home.

seventeen

BEAU

REACHER IS STILL MOPING AROUND the house. And, unless it's my imagination, Joe isn't acting his usual peppy self either. He only met her once, but she must have left a lasting impression on the horse.

Hoss couldn't care less—he doesn't give a crap about much of anything. I think he might be getting irritated with the other two though.

I don't blame them. I feel grumpier than my usual sunny self. It's ridiculous how much better I felt after just a few lines of texts last night. How does anyone stand to be separated from their person? I know families do it all the time, but I'd never thought about it before.

"What should I make for supper tonight?" Reacher answers with a snort. He's watching me from his pillow in the kitchen with his head resting on his paws. His big sad gaze stares up at me. "You have got to snap out of it, buddy. You're bringing the whole house down." He doesn't look convinced.

"Fine, you're getting your regular supper, and I'm having chili." I stop, remembering our conversation about the perfect thing for a cold winter night. "Maybe leftover meatloaf instead."

I dig through the refrigerator until I find the wrapped plate. Reba sent a whole meatloaf over yesterday. I think it's a pity meatloaf. Doesn't matter, I'll still eat it.

With my microwaved meal, I walk into the living room and flop down on the couch. There's another old movie already queued up in the player.

Soon, I should have a better selection to choose from. They come next week to install my new satellite internet. It's really more for safety than anything. Don't get the wrong idea and think it's so I can communicate with a certain someone better.

"I can't even fool myself," I explain to Reacher, who's moved to his space in front of the fireplace. He watches the lights flicker on the Christmas tree.

Yes, it's still up. Also yes, it's after New Year's Day. The tree itself looks like it's on its last leg, but I haven't had the heart to take it down. Jesus, I'm totally whipped from long distance. I'm not all that upset about that either.

After taking a bite of fucking hot meatloaf, I hit play on the remote. My gaze drifts to my phone just in case there were any texts. Nothing.

Popping another bite in my mouth because I forgot how damn hot the first one was, I refocus on the movie. At least Mom had pretty good taste in entertainment.

I'm halfway through an eighties adventure when I hear a truck pull up outside. I never get many visitors. Usually, the only traffic is package deliveries or Travis. He'd better have his ass in Austin for class tomorrow.

Pausing the movie, I open the front door. The truck has

already tossed something out and hauled ass back down the road.

Sitting on the steps is a box. I lug it inside and set it on the coffee table. The address is from somewhere in California. An idiotic grin appears on my face as I tear open the box.

Inside are layers of things. The first thing I pull out is a package full of dog toys and treats. Reacher barks excitedly as if he knows who the box is from. I toss him one of the toys.

There's a note inside that says "For the next time." I pull out several board games with a laugh. She's sent Jenga, Battleship, an Uno deck, and Clue. Farther down is a box of herbal teas—all my favorites.

Finally, I pull out a concert T-shirt with her tour dates on the back. Whipping my shirt off, I pull it over my head. It's a bit snug, but it works. I wish she could see the photos in her frames hanging on my wall. Trace sent me a whole bunch of good ones from Christmas.

"What do you think?" Reacher looks up with a snort before returning to his toy. The way he's shaking it makes me believe it'll be in pieces shortly. "Yeah, I like it to. What do you think she's up to?" Only one way to find out. Besides, I need to thank her for the presents.

Me: Got the package. Reacher is beside himself.

Harmony: And his minion?

Me: He's beside himself too.

Harmony: That's good to hear. The house must be getting crowded.

Me: You're a riot.

Harmony: I try.

Me: When do you go on next?

Harmony: Tomorrow. Just chilling tonight. Working on stuff.

Me: Stuff huh?

Harmony: Yep. Stuff.

I feel my grin growing bigger. It's ridiculous how even a few words of text from her pick my spirits up. Damn, I miss listening to her talk.

I'm amazed I'm even getting her text in the house. Last night, I climbed the hill behind the house to make sure I got a signal. That will all be in the past next week.

Harmony: How is Reacher anyway?

Me: Grumpy, Mopey, Crabby.

Harmony: And you?

Me: Grouchy, Whiney, Snarly.

Harmony: Oh my. One more and you'll have all 7 dwarfs.

Me: Are you volunteering for Snow White?

Harmony: I wish I could. Sitting on a bus all day is boring.

Me: At least you have your stuff.

Harmony: At least.

My heart aches. I knew it was possible for a heart to feel physical pain. I remember my heart hurting for months after Mom and Dad died.

Separation heartbreak is a new thing for me though. It didn't happen when Travis went to college. Maybe because I knew he was only a short drive away. Harmony, however, might as well be on the moon. I'm not even sure where she is. Somewhere on the West Coast last time I heard.

Me: Where are you headed to?

Harmony: Utah.

Me: That sounds...I don't know how that sounds.

Harmony: Me neither. I've never been to Utah before.

Me: I heard the skiing is pretty good.

Harmony: I'm only there a day before we head back out. Back to Nevada, I think.

Me: Play the slots for me.

Harmony: Fingers crossed we win a landfall.

I wonder if she won a landfall if she would keep singing. She's damn good at it, but is it what she wants, or is it just a way to make a living? I never thought to ask.

She seemed to enjoy her impromptu concert in my kitchen. I know we did. She has so much talent, I would hate to see her stop. I don't understand how she won't burn out with the schedule her label is pushing. It worries me. Have I earned the right to worry about her yet? I hope so.

Me: When do you get a break?

Harmony: I have a short one In a month.

Me: That's a long time.

Harmony: I know. Will you come see me in Dallas?

Me: I can try. Depends on what's happening here.

Harmony: I understand. I think we're stopping to eat.

Me: Okay. Be safe.

I know I sound like an asshole when I say I'll have to see what's happening. That's the thing with being a rancher, though. For the most part, I can plan out a little. That's calving season, though, so I really have to see how things are going before I can flit off to the city. It seems like there's always some reason I can't get away.

"Let's go feed," I say.

Reacher rises and stretches before following me to the mudroom. The coveralls Harmony wore still hang on one of the hooks. I haven't gotten around to putting them up yet.

I'm sure Freud would have something to say about my actions, but he's not here, so I'm not worried about it.

I open the door, and we step outside. It's still cold, but at least the snow is gone. Problem is, there is mud everywhere.

"Roll in the mud, and you can sleep in the barn," I shout as Reacher shoots past me. I had to bathe that stupid dog last night. It's not easy for both of us to fit in my shower.

He waits for me at the barn. I open the door, and he shoots in to bark at the horses. They ignore him. They learned long ago he's all bark and very little bite. He just looks intimidating.

"Hey, boys," I say in greeting. Both horses are standing inside waiting for something to eat. Pretty soon they'll be able to graze the pasture again and won't need as much feed from me. Until them, I pour them each some grain and drop more hay in the rack.

"Have either of you come up with a plan yet on how to be two places at once? I need to live in Nashville with Harmony and still work the ranch."

They both ignore me as they plow through their grain. Reacher is too busy nosing through the extra hay to pay any attention. With a sigh, I turn off the lights and head back outside. The dog races out behind me, almost knocking me over in his exuberance to explore.

I pull the door closed and debate sitting on the front porch until time for bed. Everything inside reminds me of her, but it's still too cold to be out here.

"Come on, dog. Let's go warm up. Maybe we'll just head to bed early."

He barks at something in the dark but follows me to the side of the house. I go through the motions of getting the house closed down for the night. When I'm done in the bathroom, I crawl into bed. It seems like the harder I try to fall asleep, the more restless I become.

I've never gotten used to pulling the curtains closed in my bedroom. Mom would leave them open in Travis and my room so we could watch the trees outside blow in the breeze. It still puts me to sleep faster than anything else I've found.

My gaze lands on one of the pictures of Harmony and me in the homemade frame. It's a photo of us lying on the pull-out couch. She's lying on my arm as she holds the phone out to take a selfie of us.

It's the same one I drew as a surprise present for later. I tucked it into her bag before she left. Normally I'm not so sappy, but it's a really great photo. Our hair is messy, the sheet is rumpled, and we look happy. Truly happy.

She hasn't mentioned the drawing, so I assume she hasn't dug anything out of that bag yet. I know her wardrobe on tour is planned clear down to the casual stuff she wears when she's not on stage.

She looks so beautiful it takes my breath away. My hand finds my erection under the blanket. It's how I survive now that she's gone. I could honestly jack off at least five times a day thinking about her, but I force myself to wait until bedtime.

My eyes close as I punish myself for letting her walk out my door. I know I had no choice, but sometimes I wonder if everything could be different.

I remember how she looked under me in the soft glow of the fireplace. Her soft blue eyes would turn smokey as she got close. Then she would close them as she rode out her orgasm. The one I gave her. It was a gift she let me in on every damn time.

The lazy smile as she lay in my arms after is emblazoned in my mind forever. Her responses to the things I said like muscle memory running through my body.

My efforts spill over my hand in an unsatisfactory end. This is never enough. I want to be with her. I want to roll my eyes at her movie selections, complain when she insists that I help her create some elementary school art project, and fall asleep with her soft breath on my neck. Quite simply, I've fallen in love with someone I can't have, and it's ripping me apart.

eighteen

HARMONY

"HELLO?" I say, answering a phone call from an unknown caller. My phone is so locked down it's rare I get unknown calls. It's rare for me to get phone calls at all. Most people have to go through at least Robin to get a hold of me.

"Can you hear me?" the voice says from the other end. My heart starts racing.

"Beau? Oh my gosh, is it really you?" I feel every emotion at once it seems. My palms are sweaty, my cheeks heat, and I can't get enough air. Who knew just a single voice could render me a basket case?

"Yeah, sweetheart, it is. Damn, it's good to hear your voice."

"But, how? Where are you?"

"At home. I caved to high-speed satellite internet. Didn't know how much I needed it until now." My stomach flutters. "How are you?"

"I'm so much better now," I answer. I swear I can hear

him smile over the phone. "What have you been doing? How's Reacher? And Joe and Hoss? Tell me everything!" He laughs this time.

"Everyone is good. Reacher is still moping. Hang on, I'll put you on speakerphone so he can hear you." I hear the phone click.

"Reacher, sweet baby," I purr. There's a bark at the other end. The phone clicks back over.

"That's enough from him. He'll just hog your attention, and I want it all to myself."

God, how does this man know exactly what to say? If I was there, I'd climb on his lap, rip all his clothes off and ride him like a tornado in a Kansas trailer park. I want to be with him so badly, it physically hurts.

"So, if you have fancy internet, can we video chat?" I have an idea, but I don't want to propose it here in the middle of the band on the bus.

"We can. Any time you want, just let me know so I'm not outside working."

"That means we can have—" I take a look around me. Most of the guys are in the back. Luke is sitting on one of the sofas, but he's got his headphones on. "Video sex?" Beau laughs again.

"Sure. Do I get to role play?"

"Oooh, you have me intrigued."

"Yeah, me too. I guess I'd better start working on that," he says. "I should probably get back to work. I just wanted to let you know you can get a hold of me in the evenings now. I sort of miss your yammering."

"Aww, I've started to grow on you," I tease. "I miss you too, Beau," I whisper before he ends the call.

"Is that grin from ear to ear because of that phone call?"

Luke asks. "Wouldn't be your mystery man from back home, would it?"

"Yeah," I admit, moving to the sofa across from him. "It won't last, but it's nice to have someone for now."

"Why won't it last?"

"Because he lives on his family ranch he won't leave, and I do this," I say, motioning around the bus.

"If you want something bad enough, you figure out how to make it work. Have you told him you want it to work?"

"Not really. I don't want him to give up anything for me."

"Then tell him that. Tell him you want to work this shit out." He stares at me for a long time as I scowl into space trying to envision what my life could be with Beau. "You'll never find out if you don't try." He pulls his headphones back on and begins strumming his guitar again.

He's right. I need to find the guts to tell Beau how I feel. That I've fallen hopelessly in love with him, and I'm not willing to give up on us.

I don't know if he feels the same way I do. I might be nothing more than some one-time deal. I don't think he would be calling me a month later if I were. That doesn't mean he wants to go to the extraordinary effort it's going to take to continue, though.

I don't have to do this alone. There are two men in Texas who will have my back. Travis only wants what will make Beau happy. If I make his brother happy, then I know he'll help. Picking back up my phone, I press his number in my address book.

"What's up, sunshine?" he answers. "I'm walking to class, so it'll have to be quick."

"Can you get Beau to the show in Dallas?"

"I can try."

"Can you try really, really hard. I need him to be there, Travis," I plead.

"Then I'll get him there."

"Thank you so much. I'll have tickets at the hold counter for all three of you."

"Sounds good. Gotta go. Ciao." The line goes dead. Now, I just need the song to be ready in time. I tap on Luke's knee with my foot. He pulls his headphones back off and looks over at me.

"Can we work on the new song?" I ask.

"What do you think I've been doing nonstop since I saw it? I can't get it out of my head. I think I'm humming it in my sleep now."

"That's how it started in the first place. I met Beau, and this tune started nagging my mind." I pull my guitar onto my lap. You can usually find most of our instruments sitting around the bus at any time. "Ready? I'll start, and you join in with what you're thinking." I begin the melody, and Luke jumps in on his guitar filling in the sound.

Somewhere down the bus, I hear a bass start up. It sounds odd until Kenny plugs it into the amp sitting in the living area. I guess I'm not the only one who has become obsessed with the song. Kip soon drags the small keyboard he practices on to the couch next to me.

We're doing pretty good when Chris shows up. He uses some electronic pad things in place of his drum set. It's not quite the same, but it gets the job done. We start and stop to tweak some chord or word until Robin appears.

An hour later, we have something that I think will be our first hit off the next album. Who knows, maybe it will even be our first real breakout hit. Robin declares it will, though she is the posterchild for enthusiasm.

What's important is what the label will think. And

what Beau will think. I'm nervous to think about singing it to him in front of everyone. But, if that's not a declaration of my need to be with him, I don't know what is.

The next couple of weeks seem to drag on forever. I get a small break, but between Beau's cows having their babies and my schedule, we don't get to see each other.

We don't even have time for that sexy video call I'm desperate for. I'm out every evening pitching the next album to anyone who will listen, and he's in bed early.

At least when the break is over, I know we only have a few more weeks, and then I'm done until we head into the studio. All in all, it's been a great tour. We've sold out several of the venues, and the reception of the fans has been amazing.

I'm finishing up one of the good ones right now as a matter of fact. I've just signed the last poster when Robin turns in the door.

"Do you want to change here or on the bus?" she asks.

"Can I just have a few minutes to regroup? I promise I'll be out in ten. Just a chance at a little silence."

"Sure," she answers. "I'll be down the hall. Take your time. I'll have the guys head outside."

"Thanks, Robin." I slump down on a couch and kick off my boots. Picking up my phone, I video call Beau. I just want to see his face for a few minutes before moving on. We have a long drive overnight.

"Hey, gorgeous," he says when he answers. He's sitting on the couch in his living room, and I'm knocked breathless by how homesick I am. "You look exhausted. Good show tonight?"

"Great show. We sold out."

"That's fantastic." His one eye squints as he studies me. I know he's worried about me, it's his tell. He's right, I am exhausted. "Do you have to travel tonight?"

"Yeah. We're booked tomorrow night. I hate traveling at night. It's hard to sleep on the bus for some reason."

"I can help with that," he says. His eyes grow darker, which is something because they're already remarkably dark. "Lean back on the couch and set your phone on the table if there is one in front of you."

There's not, but the makeup table isn't far away. It takes me a minute to balance my phone against the mirror and return to the couch. I lean back in anticipation. My heartbeat is through the roof.

"Is the door locked?" he asks.

I nod my head like a bobblehead.

"Good. Work that skirt up to your waist." I do so slowly. I intend to give him the show of his life. My hands shake as my eyes cut to the door.

"Now," he growls, and my gaze snaps back to the phone. He's moved his tablet to the coffee table. I can't stop from licking my lips at the view of the top button of his jeans popped open.

"Do you ache for me?" I nod again. "Show me. Show me how wet I make you." I spread my legs until he can see the dampness of my panties. "Good girl," he purrs. "Slide your fingers inside those panties." I do as he orders. "Tell me what you feel."

"I'm so slick. My clit throbs listening to your voice. Please, take it out," I whimper. He obliges me by unzipping his jeans further until he can pull his cock out into his hand.

I imagine licking the bead of precum off as his hand slowly slides up and down the length. Without conscious knowledge, I start circling my clit with my fingers.

"No," he growls. "You don't get to do that until I say. Slide those fingers inside your cunt the way I know you like it." I do so until I'm moaning. "Lick it off. Tell me how it tastes."

"Musky, like arousal and music. But also a hint of spicy like an ancient spice that's been lost to time," I describe after pulling my fingers from my mouth.

"Fuck, I should be there. You should be coming on my tongue." His fist pumps harder as he punishes himself for missing out. "Show me," he demands, his gaze never leaving mine. "Show me how you make yourself come."

I pull my panties to the side and use two fingers to make circles teasing my clit. He moans in the background. The noise only makes me move faster begging my body to give him the show he deserves and me the release I crave.

"Come for me, siren." And I do. As hard as I try, I can't keep my eyes open as wave after wave of orgasm hit me. My body quakes as the power of it surges through me.

Somewhere far away, I hear him call my name. Or maybe that's me calling his. I don't know anymore. My body releases me finally, and I slump back on the couch. My gaze finds Beau still sitting. His hand still holds his cock, but it's covered now in cum.

"Better?" he asks.

"So much better," I answer. "You?"

"Definitely." He works at wiping his hand off and buttoning his pants back up. I wish he wouldn't. I could stare at his naked body all day. "This was a brilliant idea."

"There's only one way it could be better."

"If I'd been recording it?" he teases.

"If you were here," I answer. He grins, and I end the call. They'll be banging on the door soon. I should probably be decent by then.

nineteen

BEAU

I'M STILL REELING a week later from the most amazing sexual video encounter ever when I hear someone pull up outside. I knew Harmony was a spitfire, but damn, watching her get herself off like that was on a whole different level.

It didn't make up for the fact we were both too busy to see each other during her break. It bothers me that it will continue to be a constant in our lives.

Reacher jumps up and sniffs at the door with his tail wagging furiously. I assume it's Travis. He doesn't greet anyone else, except Harmony, like that, and she's getting ready to go on stage somewhere near Kansas City. I don't bother to move from my seat on the couch as a key is inserted into the lock in the front door.

"Who's the good boy," I hear as Travis steps in the front door. He pulls a small dog cookie out of his pocket for Reacher. The dog happily trots back to the fireplace before flopping down on the floor. "You are," he adds, pointing at me.

"What are you doing here?" I roll my eyes. He ignores it.

"I've come to get you for the concert in Dallas." Shit, that's right. Harmony asked if I would still be able to go. I told her I would try my best, but with calving, I can't guarantee I can get away.

"I don't think I can go. I've had to pull two so far and sew up a prolapse. Weather has been wreaking havoc on calving this year." Believe it or not, weather really does affect how many problems arise during calving season.

"It's nearing the end. Besides, I've got that handled," he answers. He tosses his bag on the floor and sinks into the armchair. He sees me watching him with a smirk that says I don't believe him for an instant.

"I've got it. I hired Doc Mooney's grandson to come watch everything for the weekend. You remember Ross, don't ya?" Dr. Mooney has been the family veterinarian since I was a kid. His grandson grew up running around the practice.

"What, is he about a junior in high school by now?" I feel immeasurably older thinking he was just a toddler not long ago. Isn't that the first clue that you're old? Pretty soon I should be waxing poetic about the good ole days.

"Senior. He's heading off to A&M next fall to study pre-vet. He's going to stay here at the house for the weekend. Told me he'll just drive in for class. He has early release anyway." Travis watches me with his own smirk this time while I run through and reject every reason I can think of why Ross shouldn't be here instead of me.

"He's coming over tomorrow morning so you can tell him everything he already knows. Then you can micromanage by phone while we're gone."

"I don't micromanage," I grouse. He smirks again. "Maybe I do. I don't know, I've never tried it before. Maybe I micromanage like a son-of-a-bitch."

"Well, you did a damn good job with me while I was still living here," Travis says with a laugh. Did I? I don't remember. That life now feels like something I watched on television. "Besides, you can't disappoint Harmony."

I don't answer him. I would never want to disappoint Harmony, but to what end? How do we do this when we live so far apart? As amazing as it was, we can't sustain a relationship built solely on video sex. Not the kind of relationship I want anyway. I suspect Harmony will want more too.

"Don't you have class tomorrow?" I ask, trying to steer the conversation away from things I can't control. "I still have no problem beating you bloody for skipping class."

"Whoa there, Dad. I've already gotten clearance to miss tomorrow. Speaking of, I need to talk to you about school anyway."

"You'd better not be thinking of quitting," I growl. My eyes narrow at him as he shifts in his chair to face me.

"I'm not quitting. Besides, I'm a grown-ass man, you can't stop me if that's what I decide."

"Try me." I glare at him until he finally rolls his eyes.

"I'm not quitting, but I've been thinking of after graduation. I only have one year left after this semester." Somehow, he managed to do all of his undergraduate in three years. He had busted his ass every summer to work in extra classes so he could enter law school early. He takes a deep breath. "I'm thinking of coming back here after graduation."

"What?"

"Well, not here exactly. But I've been talking to a firm in

Fredericksburg about joining them after graduation while I work on the bar exam. They've already offered me an internship this summer."

He grows quiet, and I sit back to consider what he's saying. It doesn't make any sense. He's smart enough to become a big attorney for some high-powered firm in a city. His grades have been exemplary. He's even at the top of his class. I know there are a million questions I should ask him, but I can only think of one.

"Why?"

"Because," he starts. He stops and considers me with a sigh. "Because I want to come home. I want to be here for you this time." I open my mouth to protest, but he holds up a hand to stop me. "It's your turn, Beau. I don't think anyone could ask for a better brother. You were there to pick up the pieces when Mom and Dad died, but I'm not a kid anymore.

"I want you to do what you want in life, not just what is expected. If that's living out here like a grouchy hermit the rest of your life, so be it. But I saw the way you looked at Harmony. I've seen you with a girlfriend before, but I've never seen you look at them the way you did her. You fell in love, don't deny it.

"If Harmony is who you want to be with, then I want to help. It's not as impossible as you think it is. She was always the nicest person in school. She never made me feel less than everyone else. I think she fell in love with you, too, because deep under your grumpy ways, she knows what a good guy you are." He stops to see if what he's saying is sinking in. It is, little by little.

"First," I say. "I stayed because it was the best thing for both of us. I've never regretted that decision."

"I know," he says quietly.

"Do you? Do you understand that nothing I did was ever a burden? You're not just my brother, you're my best friend. I would make every decision the exactly the same if I had it to do over." I watch him study the carpet in front of him.

"Except for hooking up with your classmate that first year of law school that weekend. That deserved a better decision." He laughs, and his gaze meets mine.

"What about Trace?" I ask.

"He's coming with me. His grandpa has agreed to front the money for a small restaurant in Fredericksburg. He'll finally get to run his own place. He said he'll even learn to, and I quote, 'get along those little dogies or whatever y'all do.'"

We both laugh. Trace had to grow on me slowly, but I think he's perfect for my brother now.

"Well, I'm not going to tell you what to do. That's a decision you have to make on your own. I will admit, however, that it would be nice to have you around again."

"So, I can stay here this summer while I intern?"

"It's your room. Hell, this is half your ranch."

"Trace, too, on the days he comes here to visit?"

"Sure."

"And what about where Harmony will stay when she's here?" I study him closely. There's no doubt in his eyes that I can work it out with her.

"She's not staying in your room, I can guarantee that."

"I'll bring noise canceling headphones." He grins at me. I shake my head. Jesus, this kid. "Now, how do we convince Harmony this can work?"

"I have no idea. I haven't even convinced myself yet."

"We need a plan," he says. We both fall silent again trying to work out a logical plan. "Let's figure out what she would need to stay here part of the year and what you need to live in Nashville part of the time. Then how you would handle touring. Can you handle spending time in Tennessee?"

"Yeah, I've only been there once, but I liked it. Same laidback pace as here. I'm sure I could figure it out, but what happens here when I'm gone?"

"That's what we have to figure out. First let's work on Harmony's list, then we'll tackle yours. I think top priority would be a studio."

"How would I do that?" I ask. It's not like the house has hidden rooms we haven't used yet. My office would never be big enough for her, and there are only two bedrooms.

"I know a guy, or more accurately, I know the wife of a guy. I'll give you her number."

By the time we realize it's way past when I usually go to bed, we have a workable plan. It still sounds a little impossible to me, but I've promised Travis to try.

I really want it to work. He insists the first step to put the plan into motion is to show up for the concert tomorrow night. With the arrangements already made for a fill-in, I can't refuse.

Ross shows up as promised to get familiar with the ranch. He's been here before when his grandpa made a farm call, but I still show him around. He pays attention better than most high school kids I've dealt with. Reacher even greets him amicably enough, so I'm not too worried about them getting along.

Before I have a chance to protest, Travis has me packed into his car and headed for Dallas. I suggested that I drive myself so he doesn't have to bring me back. He wouldn't hear of it. I think he's worried I'll change my mind halfway there and turn around.

Okay, he's not wrong. It is a consideration. Not only am I a little nervous about seeing Harmony again, I'm worried about Ross getting in over his head.

"You know his grandpa can help, if necessary, right?" Travis asks before we've gotten very far down the road. "The man is your vet." I'm not sure when he began reading my mind, but it's irritating.

"Did I say anything?" I snarl.

"Dude, I can see the smoke coming out of your ears from here. I swear everything will be fine. Try to focus on what's ahead. Step one, show up for her and declare your undying love," he answers.

"This isn't *High School Musical* or whatever shit you've been watching."

"First off, I have not been watching old made for TV movies, though Zac Effron can still rock that body. You're not the only asshole who reads in this family." He snorts in what can only be derision. "You should pick up a romance novel once in a while. Might actually learn something."

"I can hear your bodice ripping from here."

"You're a jerk, you know that," he fires back, but he's grinning. He shoves my shoulder with his hand. I smile as I straighten back up. "How far can we drive before you need another coffee."

"I've got my travel mug," I answer, shaking the tumbler at him. "We're good until lunch."

"Good, there's a place in Waco I want to try. Bladder can hold until then?"

"How old do you think I am?"

"Just asking. No need to get all huffy. I mean, you do go to bed by nine, so..."

"Bite me."

"There's the man my beautiful blonde friend fell for." He laughs. I turn to sulk out the window, but I can't do it for very long.

Just the thought that Harmony might feel for me the way I do for her makes me smile. Travis catches me grinning like an idiot out the window. This time, though, instead of teasing me, he just smiles back.

twenty

HARMONY

I'VE NEVER GOTTEN nervous about walking out on stage before. The butterflies in my stomach have always been attributed to excitement not nerves.

For the first time ever, I'm worried. What if Beau doesn't come, or what if I'm wrong, and he isn't interested in a relationship at all? What if he just wants a casual thing? Can I really do casual? Do I even want to?

My fingers strum my guitar mindlessly while I wait off stage to be announced. I wish Travis had let me know what's happening on his end. We rehearsed the entire song earlier, so I know that will be okay. I just wish I could look into a crystal ball and see the future.

"He's going to like it, sweetheart," Luke says, stepping up next to me. "And if he doesn't, he doesn't deserve you." I smile because it's a sweet thing to say, but it does nothing to calm my nerves. "Are you about ready?"

"Yeah, I'm good."

"Okay, see you out there." The band walks out onto

stage to a rowdy response. I can already tell this is going to be a good night as far as the audience goes. I hear my name and plaster on my best smile. Stepping out on stage, I wave to the crowd. It looks packed tonight.

"Hello, Dallas!" I say into the microphone. "Thank you for joining us tonight." Desperately I squint into the crowd. I wouldn't see Beau through the stage lights even if he was standing in front of me. Doesn't stop me from trying though. "Here's one I think you'll recognize." Chris starts up a beat on the drums before the rest of us join in.

We always start with the first single off our recent album to get the crowd going. Through the lights, I see people singing along, swaying to the beat, and cheering. None, as far as I can tell, is Beau. I push all thoughts of him out of my mind. I need to focus on giving our fans the best show I can.

When the song is done, we roll right into the next one. I don't speak again until after it's finished. On the floor is taped our playlist with marks to show when I change costumes and speak.

I change shortly off stage while the band plays some instrumentals, then it's right back on. The song comes to an end, and I rush off stage. Robin is there to make sure everything goes as planned.

I began the concert in a traditional country dress covered in rhinestones. The next outfit, though, is my favorite. It's my ode to the very person who put me here in the first place, Kelly Clarkson.

I slide the skin-tight leather pants up my legs. The silver studded belt has already been run through the loops, so all I have to do is hook it. With a sleeveless graphic cropped T-shirt and flashy pair of boots, I'm ready.

"Everyone," I say into the microphone handed to me.

"Luke Masters on lead guitar." I point to him. He does a riff, and the crowd cheers. Each band member follows suit as I introduce them. "As for me, I'm Harmony Ellis." We launch into a great number that Luke and Kenny wrote. The beat just makes you want to get up off that couch and dance I say.

That's how the rest of the evening goes. We play, I sing, I change clothes, and talk to the audience. It's a lot of fun. I've almost forgotten about the song I wrote until Luke nods at me.

Picking up my guitar, I climb onto the stool one of the stage crew brings me. Here goes nothing. Either he's here, or he's not. Either he takes the words to heart, or he doesn't.

"This song has never been heard before outside of the band. I started writing it when I was snowed in back home over the holidays. It's the brand, new single coming out on the new album next year." I clear my throat and begin to play. The fans grow almost spooky silent as my voice fills the venue.

I sing for all I'm worth as the band joins in. The song is sweet and a little melancholy. It's about how my home is not a place but a certain man I know. How he looks at me with his dark gaze, and I know I'm more than enough.

It talks about how he treats me like I'm the most amazing person in the world, and how, when I'm in his arms, everything else melts away. It's a song about love, devotion, respect, and longing.

I can see several people in the crowd wipe at their eyes. I guess they know the feeling I get when I'm with him.

The song ends, and there's a quiet moment before the fans go wild. I honestly don't care if they like it or not, I wrote it for one person. I take a bow and disappear off stage. There's no way I can stay for an encore song tonight. I'm too raw. The band will fill in for me. Handing my guitar to one of the stagehands, I head for my dressing room.

"You have a handful of fans," Robin says quietly. "That was beautiful by the way."

"Can you give me a minute before showing them in?" She nods and backs out of the room. I take the minute to get a drink of water, carefully dab the sweat off my face, and change from the last sparkly outfit back into something comfortable but fan-worthy. Yep, another pair of tight pants and a sleeveless crop top. Hey, I learned from the best.

"Ready?" Robin asks, sticking her head in the door. I can still hear the band playing as the first fans come through the door. The guys will be back downstairs in a minute to meet them too.

I smile and thank them through the gushing. I wonder what they'd think if they could see me with greasy hair, curled up on Beau's couch, with a giant dog in my lap.

"I thought your last song was so good," a teenage girl says. She's cute in her cowboy boots and short skirt. "You said it was about a boy? Who?"

"You'll just have to wait and see," I tease. "Thank you. I'm so glad you liked it."

Her mother snaps several pictures of us, and I take at least three selfies. After signing her poster, I sent them on to talk to the rest of the band. More people crowd into the dressing room. No sign of Beau or Travis. I thought at the very least Trace would be here.

"There she is!" I hear finally as the line thins. Travis walks in and throws his arms around me. I'm spun until I think I'm going to blow.

"Travis!" I exclaim, and he sets me back on my feet. "Trace." Trace is standing behind Travis shaking his head.

"Sweetheart, that was beyond," he says. "We would have been here sooner, but I had to wait for Trav to stop sobbing in the bathroom."

"Lies," Travis says with a grin. "I did have to blow my nose though. God, I had no idea that was in your head when we showed up Christmas Day."

"It really is something," Trace agrees.

"An instant hit. I can't wait for the new album." I appreciate them building up my ego, but there's only one thing I want to know.

"Did Beau hear it? Is he here?" Okay, that's two, so sue me.

"Maybe you should see for yourself." I follow Travis out of the dressing room, and leaning against the wall like he's waiting for a bus is the man I've been dreaming about.

Words that seemed to come so easily normally fail me as I gaze at him. He's even more beautiful than I remember. He pushes off the wall and uncrosses his arms. They fall to his sides.

"Yeah, we're going to head off. Great concert, Harmony." Trace grabs Travis's hand, and they head down the hallway.

"Hi," I manage to get out.

"Hi," he answers. "That song was about me?" I nod. "That's what Travis said. I don't think anyone has ever seen me as their home."

"I'm not just anyone," I answer.

"You certainly aren't." He stares down the hallway for a second before turning back to me. The rest of the band steps into the hallway. They introduce themselves, and Beau shakes hands in turn.

"You good here?" Luke asks.

"She's good," Beau says before I can answer.

"Okay, talk later. Nice to meet you." They walk down the hallway until there's only the two of us left. Beau looks back down at me.

"What do you want to do?" He's not asking a simple question about tonight. I can tell by the steady gaze that he truly wants to know where we go from here.

"I want to come home," I say. His hand reaches out and wraps behind my neck. Slowly, he draws me closer to him. Bending, he whispers in my ear.

"Then come home." I don't need more. Beau says nothing he doesn't mean. Nothing this important anyway.

I can't stand it anymore. I have to be as close to him as possible. Throwing my arms around him, I jump. He pulls me up around his waist, and I'm kissing him before either of us can say another word.

"I love you, Harmony," he says when our kiss settles from its fevered pitch. His words are so raw that I know they're not said in haste. "I don't understand how or when, but I know I've fallen in love with you. I can figure out how to make this work if you can help me."

"I love you, Beau. I'll do whatever I have to, as long as I'm with you." His dark gaze searches my face. "I don't want to do all of this without you anymore."

He nods, his eyebrows drawing down like he's been given a mission. Maybe he has because I don't know how we'll make this work either. But if he needs time to work it out, then he can have it in spades. I'm not going anywhere.

"Should we get out of here?" He sets me back on my feet. "Do we need to get your stuff?"

"Robin will deal with it."

"What about your bag? Do you have clothes with you?"

"I don't plan on needing clothes tonight."

"I like how you think," he says with a smile. Sliding his hand into mine, he pulls me down the hallway.

It's a short ride to his hotel. Then he's opening the door to his room. My skin erupts in goose bumps with anticipation. We only have tonight before I'm on the bus again heading to our next stop. I intend to get very little sleep.

"Did you ever find your other Christmas present I put in your suitcase?" he asks, walking through the door.

"No, I haven't even looked in that case since Christmas. What is it?" It's torture to tell someone they have a surprise gift when they can't open it that minute. The first thing I'm doing when I get back to the bus is dragging it out from the belly and ripping it open. "Seriously, what is it?" He just grins at me. "You're killing me, you know that?"

"And you're killing me."

I squeal when he tosses me onto the bed.

"I should shower," I protest. "I'm sweaty and gross." He studies me for a beat.

"Good idea, let's shower."

I raise up on my elbows as he partially unbuttons his shirt and pulls it over his head. I'm not about to miss the show. He catches me watching and slows down. No complaints here.

That bulge threatening to escape has my mouth watering. He kicks his boots off and makes a show of shimming out of his jeans.

"Now it's your turn," he says when there's nothing left of his clothes to remove.

I can't stop from appreciating his hard length standing proudly between us, begging for attention. Before I can reach for it, he takes the hem of my shirt in both hands and pulls it over my head. I have no idea where it lands when he tosses it over his shoulder.

He presses me down until I'm lying flat on the bed so he can pull my pants down my legs. His hands brush up my inner thighs making me shiver as he returns for my panties. The growl he makes leads me to think he likes the barely-there lace thong I chose. My back arches as he moves to unhook my bra.

In one smooth movement, he stands back up, pulls me from the bed to his shoulder, and walks into the shower. I would squeal and protest, but honestly, it was a pretty badass move.

The sound of the shower is something I can only hear until he steps inside. Water hits my ass in a sheet. I'm starting to get lightheaded from being upside down.

"Still on birth control?" he asks.

"Yep." He swings me up and slowly lowers me down his body.

"This isn't going to be slow," he warns. Our gazes meet as he holds me close to his chest. His throbbing cock teases my entrance until I nod in agreement. Then I'm impaled on him in one hard thrust.

"Beau," I cry out. I'm not sure if it's the sudden fullness or the overwhelming emotions, but I cling to him desperately.

"You're okay." It isn't a question, it's a demand. "Take it all." How does he drive me to madness with just his words?

He gives me only a moment to adjust before he's thrusting into me in a punishing rhythm. He's right though. I am okay. I'm better than okay.

"Harder," I beg.

"You think you can take it harder?" he growls.

"Yes."

"Then beg for it, little girl. Beg for every inch."

"Please," is all I can get out. He's right, this isn't going to be slow. I can feel it building deep in my core. The coils threading through my body chasing a high only he can give me.

I lose myself in the delicious friction of his lower abs against my clit as he pounds even harder. Turns out, I didn't need to beg. He knows exactly what I need and gives it to me.

"Beau!" I scream as the waves crest and break over.

Silently, I beg my mind to hold me forever in this place. To never let me leave. I don't think it's possible to live in that world, though, without losing your mind. So, my body betrays me as it brings me back to earth. Beau holds me tight as my senses return.

"Jesus," he murmurs. I couldn't agree more.

twenty-one

BEAU

YOU WOULD THINK LEAVING Harmony at the bus the day after the concert would be the worst thing I would ever do.

In reality, it wasn't that bad. I know she'll be here the moment the tour wraps up, which gives me something to look forward to. Besides, she rode me so hard and so often that night that I woke up sore. My abs needed a rest. Not complaining, just stating a fact.

I've got my hands full anyway. The Ross kid worked well while I was in Dallas, so I've hired him on the weekends to help around the ranch. It frees me up a little to get some things done before Harmony comes home.

Jesus, I never thought someone would think of me as their home. I plan to be the best damn home she could ever hope for. It's why I'm walking into the library on a Friday afternoon.

"Beau Rayburn!" Austen, the head librarian, exclaims. "I

haven't seen you in a hot minute. Heard you've been keeping busy." She elbows me in the ribs.

I've only known Austen as the librarian even though she grew up here too. Her older sister, Eliot, was a freshman when I was a senior, I think. I remember something about her being pretty smart.

"Hey, Austen. I see the rumor mill is continuing to spin."

"Small towns," she answers with a shrug. "What can you do?"

"That's why I'm here actually. Travis gave me the number for your younger sister. Something about her husband being a contractor or such? Anyway, it seems weird calling her up. I thought you might have his number?"

"I can do you one better. They're in town this week, just go bang on their door. They live in that old house the Harrels owned when we were kids. The one with the porch on the front down from the Catholic church," she says.

"Yeah, I know it. I don't want to bug them though."

"You're not going to bug them. Besides, a little bugging will do Brontë good. What are you doing anyway?"

"Some remodeling, but I need plans done."

"Oooh, is it for Harmony?" she asks. I can't stop the smile when I hear her name. "Good for you," she adds, thwacking my stomach. "Hey, if you need any landscaping too, give Reed a call. I'll grab his card for you." She flits off to her office.

I forgot she married Reed Campbell. All I really remember of him in high school was he was a hell of a base-ball player. Seems like the girls were all giggling over him in the halls too.

"Here you go," she says, reappearing by my side. I take

the proffered card and slide it into my shirt pocket. I can't imagine needing landscaping at the ranch, but you never know. "Let me know if you need anything else." With a small wave, she walks toward a group of giggling girls at one of the tables.

Staring up at the house Austen's sister owns from the seat of my truck takes me by surprise. It takes some effort to remember what it looked like when I was a kid. The remodel is epic.

I might as well get this meeting over with. I'm not sure they'll take the job since it's so small, but I won't know if I don't ask.

"Hi," a stunning woman says, opening the door before I'm even halfway up the steps. "I'm Brontë, and this is Keats," she says, referring to a toddler clutched in her arms. "Austen just called and said you were heading this way. I knew Travis in school, and I remember something about an older brother, but that seems like a lifetime ago."

"Beau," I say, introducing myself.

"That's right. Well, please come in, Beau. Rand is trying to wrap up a phone call in his office. Can I get you something to drink while you wait?"

"No, ma'am. I'm fine."

"Okay then. Have a seat, and Rand will be right out. If you'll excuse us, I need to get Keats his afternoon snack. He just woke up and gets grumpy like his dad if he doesn't get something to eat." She pushes into the kitchen, and I'm left on my own in their living room. Which looks like something out of a magazine.

I move to the fireplace to study the rockwork. This would be a nice touch in the living room. Get rid of the old brick one.

"Sorry about that," a man says, stepping out of a door.

"I'm Rand. Austen said something about some design work you need done."

"Yes, I'd like to build a music studio, but it needs more than just some construction."

"Where is this studio going?"

"In an old barn?" I don't know why I phrase it as a question, except I don't know if it's even doable.

"That sounds interesting. I tell you what. How soon do you need it done?"

"As soon as possible. My girlfriend will be back in about a month."

"Harmony Ellis, right?"

"Right." How does everyone in this town already know about us? Also, it feels crazy to call her my girlfriend. She is, but it just feels weird.

"Okay, Peter needs a couple days out of the office. How about we come see it tomorrow afternoon?" Rand asks.

"That would be great. I wasn't sure you'd even be interested."

"You kidding? We definitely want to be able to say we built the studio that took the local girl from a star to a superstar. Besides, anything to help out a brother." He winks at me. "Do you mind a local crew?"

"No, that's fine."

"Great. We'll be there tomorrow after lunch." I give him the location and head back outside.

Doubts about this whole thing begin to set in before I even make it back to my truck. I think I'm more worried about what crew he shows up with more than anything. It will be worth it, though, if it keeps Harmony with me.

· · ·

True to his word, it's not long after lunch the next day when a fancy SUV comes bumping down the dirt road to the house. Rand steps out of the driver's door. A man I don't know and a half scary-looking woman climb from the other side. I open the door to greet them, and Reacher pushes past me before I can stop him.

"Hey, big fella," the other man says, bending down. Reacher, of course, knows a dog person when he sees one. The dog presses against the man rubbing on him like he's going to produce a genie.

"Beau," Rand says, stepping forward. "This is my associate, Peter." I shake his hand briefly before he goes back to scratching Reacher's ears. "And this is my other associate and sister, Geneva."

"Or associate is plenty." She rolls her eyes as she steps forward to shake my hand. I think I've misjudged her. We might be the same side of the coin.

"Can I get you anything to drink?" I offer.

"We're good," she answers for all of them. "Show us this barn."

"It's a little rough," I say as I lead them over. It's warm enough now so both horses are out in one of the pasture traps. Pushing open the door, I lead them inside. Peter stands just inside the door taking it in while the other two start poking around. "This is the only space I can come up with."

"What's up there?" Geneva asks, pointing to the hayloft over our heads.

"Storage mostly."

"I think he needs an apartment up there for the band to stay in when they come to work," she says.

"Band?" I ask. Crap, I hadn't even thought about that. They will need somewhere to stay if they need to rehearse here or record anything. I can't exactly put them up at the house of horrors we refer to as the hotel in Dansboro Crossing. Although I guess the Elvis room could be inspiring.

"I think we have enough room that we can do a music and an art studio. I have one of your pieces on my office wall," Geneva says.

"Really, which one?" Peter asks.

"The sketch of the Pennybacker Bridge at sunset."

"Ohh, I like that one. You're right, he needs a studio also." I feel like I'm no longer in control of this project. I like the direction it's taking though. A studio where I could work in the evening while listen to Harmony would be perfect. They continue to make plans while I fantasize about the fun we could have with a couch on my side of the studio.

"Okay, we'll take it," Rand says. "I'll shoot you some preliminaries and price estimates next week. In the meantime, start emptying the loft out. We'll need to start soon to make it in a month."

"Really?" Honestly, I didn't think I could make this happen.

"It's going to be one for the magazines," Geneva announces before swooping out of the barn. We follow her slowly to the SUV where she already sits waiting.

"We'll be in touch," Rand says, grasping my hand again.

"I'll be back tomorrow to get some measurements," Peter adds, handing me his business card.

They jump in the vehicle and head back down the road. I think they were here about fifteen minutes, but they have me excited to get started. I can't wait to get in the hayloft and start cleaning. There's no telling what's up there.

"Let's go, boy. We've got our work cut out for us tomorrow," I say, walking up the steps to the house.

Reacher follows me through the door and flops down on the floor. He's just tired from trying to suck up to the architect. Fair to say, he wants Harmony here as much as I do. I still have half a day's work to do, though. I'm changing into my boots in the mudroom when my phone rings.

"I can't believe it took me this long to find this sketch," Harmony says. She doesn't mince words. "You should have told me sooner."

"Do you like it?"

"Do I like it? Do I like it?"

"Well?"

"I freaking love it!" she squeals. "It's going on the wall of our bedroom." I smile stupidly at the words rolling off her tongue. Our bedroom. "I'm going to see it every morning when I wake up and every evening before I fall asleep. I don't know how you did it."

"It's just a sketch."

"Pfft," she snorts. "It's beautiful. Thank you. Shit, I've got to go. Love you."

"Love you too," I say, but she's already ended the call.

The smile stays in place as I finish pulling on my boots. It stays all the way to where Ross is working on repairing some fence. He doesn't ask. I like this kid more all the time. He's not one for idol chit chat either.

"What'd they say?" he finally asks.

"It's doable," I answer. "Measuring tomorrow."

"Good deal." He bends back over his work. "Oh, got a date tonight. Cool, if I head out a little early?"

"Yeah, go. I've got it." He doesn't even say goodbye as he heads off. Good and quiet. My kind of person.

There's one exception, and she just yelled a curse word at me and hung up. I laugh. Thankfully, no one's around to hear me. They'd think I'd gone nuts. Maybe I have. If so, it's all because of a woman. One that likes to chatter my ear off. One I can't wait to see again.

Now I'm starting to think that some landscaping wouldn't be such a horrible idea. Some nice flowers around the house would be a welcome addition. Jesus! I'm completely whipped. Do I care? Not really. I return to the house and find the business card Austen gave me sitting on my desk.

"Go for Reed," the man on the other end says when the call connects. I roll my eyes. I've always heard the Caraway sisters were kind of crazy, but apparently the men they chose are right up there with them. Except the sheriff, he seems like a good guy.

"I'm interested in getting a quote for some landscaping."

"Groovy. I've got tomorrow afternoon open. I can come out then." Groovy? Who says that anymore?

"That works." I give him directions and end the call. Jesus, help me. What have I done?

twenty-two

BEAU

I'M OFFICIALLY in over my head.

Cleaning out the loft was hard enough. Travis showed up to help, so it didn't take as long as I thought it would.

We employed the hoarder's method of using three piles. One to keep, like Travis's baby blanket made by our grandmother who died not long after he was born. A different pile to throw away, as in my old football cleats. Nasty. And that last one for maybe, but we don't know. In other words, our elementary school art projects.

The hardest part was figuring out where to store all the stuff left since the loft was about to be turned into living quarters for guests. A lot of the stuff is now stacked in the closet of Travis's old room until I can find somewhere better for it. Preferably at his house one day.

Now there are people buzzing around my once tranquil world like it's Dansboro Crossing's newest attraction.

Peter sent over the plans two days after they saw the barn. There were a few tweaks here and there, but for the most part, they were perfect. Construction began the same week I approved them.

I guess it never occurred to me how many guys from town had pretty decent construction skills. Reed has been here since the beginning splitting his time between installing a few low-maintenance flowerbeds and Sheet rocking. He's very chatty also. I might have been signed up for a softball team too without realizing it.

Travis and Trace showed up again having taken my "emergency only" credit card to the home store in Austin. I'm now the proud owner of a new duvet and sheet set. I drew the line on throw pillows for the bed however. Why would I want to constantly be removing pillows from the bed before I get in it at night?

I did relent and keep the ones they bought for the couch. I'm also the new owner of matching wine glasses. As if I'm suddenly going to develop a wine habit.

I'm contemplating the cheery welcome mat that showed up on my doorstep when I wasn't paying attention when I hear footsteps behind me.

"Hey," Reed says.

I turn around to find him and Rand standing at the bottom of the steps.

"We're officially done. Ready for the unveiling."

I roll my eyes, but they just laugh.

"Does that mean you want to forgo the blindfold?"

"You can try," I growl. They both laugh again. I follow them across the yard to the barn. From the outside you can't really tell much was done, except for the new windows on top.

"Drum roll, please."

"Just open the door."

Reed obliges, and damn! This is definitely not the same barn I started with.

"Holy shit," I whisper, looking around.

"So, I take it you approve so far?" Rand says.

I ignore him as I step farther into the first room. It's larger than I thought possible. There's a recording booth, an area they can practice as a band, and even couches to lounge on.

Luke helped me with the design and recording equipment. I didn't even have to threaten him not to tell Harmony. He understood immediately that I wanted all of this to be a surprise.

On the other side of the window is my studio. It's filled with my art supplies, canvases, and even a place to work in other mediums. I've been debating trying my hand at sculpting, so I needed plenty of room. There's also a couch and chairs in this room, but they're covered so I don't have to worry about charcoal or paint smudges.

"Stop gaping and come upstairs," Geneva says from the stairway. I like her more and more. It's probably the award-winning personality. It matches mine. I leave the studio space to climb the stairs behind her.

Brontë's done an amazing job designing the space. They managed to carve three small bedrooms and two bathrooms out of the loft. It also has a small kitchenette and living area. Perfect for the band.

"Well?" Geneva asks when I return from looking around. Reed and Rand have joined her, all waiting for my approval.

"It's fucking brilliant," I answer. They have my approval in spades.

"I knew I liked you."

"What's not to like?" She raises an eyebrow at me. "I mean the place, not me."

"Whatever you have to tell yourself." She pulls a chair out and sits at the table. "Now to settle the bill." I close my eyes as she sets the paperwork in front of me. When I open them again, Rand is sitting next to her. Reed seems to have disappeared. My eyes stare down at the final figure. Hold on.

"This is like half of what I thought it would be," I say.

"This covers materials and outside labor. We've already explained the design costs were waved in lieu of advertising. Saying we designed the studio for Harmony Ellis is enough. Don't think we won't come knocking on your door, though, looking for an endorsement later." She takes my check with a wink. It's both a promise and a threat. If I didn't know better, I'd say we were twins separated at birth.

I don't rise from the table until I hear the last vehicle pull off down the road. Taking one last look around, I climb down the steps to the music room. Reacher is stretched out on the couch.

"That's a bad habit she let you get away with," I tease him. "Do you think she'll like it?" I ask a little more seriously. He harrumphs at me in response. "I get there's only one way to find out. How they got it done before she gets here tomorrow, I have no idea." The dog rolls over on his back with his feet braced on the back of the couch.

"These are pretty comfy," I admit, sliding down on the other couch. "Where do you think she is?" I punch in one of the few numbers in my speed dial.

"Hey, sexy. What's up?" Somehow, just hearing her voice makes my anxiety lessen. I can't wait until she fills the house with banter.

"Sitting here thinking about you."

"You always know just what to say. I think you're flirting skills have hit master level."

"I have the best test subject."

She laughs, and my heart does a flip. No one told me that being in love meant you stayed on this roller coaster of emotions all the time. Sometimes, I swear just the sound of her voice makes my skin tingle. And when we're apart, my heart feels like it's going to rip from my chest. I love the way she makes me feel inside regardless of what's happening in our lives.

"Where are you?" I ask.

"I'm about to check into a hotel in Texarkana. Don't worry, it's got all the bells and whistles including security." She's already aware of how much I worry about her. I offered to fly up and drive her here, but she insisted she come alone. I think she wants time to decompress from the road. I can respect that. "I think I'm ordering room service, taking a long bath, and falling into bed."

"Send me where you are so I don't have to stress about it all night. Do you want me to order you something in?" Travis introduced me to the joys of restaurant delivery apps last time I was in Austin. They don't do me much good here, but I'm willing to test it out for Harmony.

"No, room service will work. I've been snacking all the way here anyway, so I'm not very hungry. You know how road trips work."

"I do. Okay, text me when you get in your room."

"Yes, daddy."

"Tomorrow night, you can call me that." She giggles. "Get some rest. I can't wait until you get here."

"I love you, Beau Rayburn."

"I love you, Harmony Ellis. Sleep well." We say good

night and end the call. Tomorrow. How am I going to survive until I have her in my arms tomorrow?

"How do you feel about a rousing game of Jenga?" Reacher just grunts in response. "You're not a very social dog, you know that?"

With a sigh, I heave myself off the couch. I take a second to look around one last time, then whistling for the dog, head to the house. Tomorrow seems like forever.

I slept in fits last night tossing and turning until well after midnight. With any luck, caffeine will help. At least with the headache that's sitting right behind my eyes. It would help more if Reacher wasn't standing a foot away from where I'm leaning against the counter. He must know something is up because he's barking at me.

"How about you go outside for a while?" How about we both go outside for a while. Taking the mug of black coffee, I lead the way to the front porch.

Reed decided I needed legitimate porch furniture. I try out the new all-weather loveseat with striped cushions. He might have been on to something. It's not bad.

"Go," I growl at the dog when he continues to stand on the porch. He's looking down the road waiting. He knows what today is. "Go. Find something to terrify in the wild," I try again.

Finally, with a backward glance, he prances down the steps. He sniffs along the road for a few minutes before heading for the barn.

I understand how he feels. We're both ready to have Harmony back in our lives again. I've tried to explain to him that she plans to leave Texarkana at eight hoping to avoid rush hour in Dallas. Good luck with that, it's always rush hour in Dallas. With that in mind, I suspect it will be around two or three before we see her.

That didn't prevent me from getting up at the ass crack of dawn to pace the floor waiting for her. I check my watch for the twentieth time. It's still too early to text or call.

She sounded exhausted last night, so it's best I wait for her to contact me. Still, I can't help but worry. I should have insisted on driving her. There's a lot to learn about this boyfriend designation.

"How about we saddle up one of the horses and check water troughs?" I ask Reacher when he returns to flop at my feet. "It'll be better than waiting around here slowly going out of my mind." I return to the kitchen to wash out my mug with Reacher on my heels. My phone pings while I'm setting the mug in the drainer to dry.

Harmony: Decided to get an earlier start. I'm too ready to see you to waste any more time here.

Me: I agree. Reacher is all up in arms waiting for you.

Harmony: What about his owner?

Me: He might be a little too.

Harmony: Just a little?

Me: A lot.

Harmony: That's better. See you soon.

Me: Be careful and let me know when you stop for lunch.

Harmony: Yes, Dad.

Me: Where's the ass-spanking emoji?

She sends me a slew of dirty ones, and I laugh. I can't imagine not having her in my life now. Everything before seems so black and white. Now, I see the world in all its vivid colors.

I pull on my boots by the mudroom door and step

outside. It's a perfect day for her to come home. I don't have fields of bluebonnet because they're actually poisonous to cattle, but I know they line the roads right now. Even the flowers welcome her home.

Reacher and I try our best to stay busy. Of course, there is not a thing wrong with any of the troughs. Ross has made sure of that. He'll be leaving for college at the end of the summer. I'm not worried though. Turns out he has a younger brother who started showing up with him to help. He's already expressed an interest in taking over when Ross leaves.

I make sure I'm around the house when Harmony stops for lunch. There's no way I'm missing that call. We only have a couple more hours before she pulls through the gate. It seems like every minute on the clock now takes hours. Is this what it will feel like every time we're apart? Reacher joins me as I stand on the front porch watching.

My eyes squint as I see a small wisp of dust in the distance. It's enough to send my heart racing. I'll never survive if that's anyone but her. The dust trail grows a little larger until, finally, a candy-apple red SUV pulls up in front of the house.

Her smile is the first thing I see as she gazes through the front windshield at us. Finally, she's come home.

HARMONY - ONE YEAR LATER

"HELLO, AUSTIN!" I yell, stepping onto the stage. It seems like I've lived a lifetime since I've said that. Little did I know the last time would lead me to where I am now.

This time, I say it with a little more gusto. It's the last time I'll be on this stage for a while—any stage. When the proverbial curtain closes tonight, I'm taking a much-needed six-month break.

My gaze casts briefly to the man standing just off stage. His arms are folded over his chest, and there's a scowl on his face. Most people can't see, however, the warmth in his eyes. I can. I can see past his concern for me as I stride out in my boots to begin the first song. I can see the love he envelops my soul in.

To say our newest album has taken off would be an understatement. Uploads of our performance in Dallas were lighting up social media before we even walked off stage.

Then our fans found out about the man in my life. Poor

Beau. He had his life splashed across every site almost overnight. It never seemed to bother him much though. I guess if there are no skeletons in your closet, you can still sleep easy at night.

About the time life in our sleepy, little world calmed down again, he proposed. It was the most romantic thing ever. We packed a picnic and spent the day by the river. He lit a fire as the sun dropped and, with the sunset in the background, got down on one knee. I knew he was a romantic at heart.

I accepted of course. Not in some beautiful, graceful way. I sobbed tears into his shirt until I broke out in hiccups. Thankfully, that didn't make the rounds on social media.

Instead, there were a million shots of his grandmother's gorgeous engagement ring on my finger. I haven't taken it off since. Our wedding was perfect with just family and friends.

Let me be the first to explain how incredibly hot a sexy cowboy looks in a tuxedo. Our wedding night in a fancy hotel in Austin was a challenge. I had a hard time deciding if I should simply marvel at him looking like something I'd like to lick or actually ripping the tux off and doing just that.

I did the latter. I'm no idiot.

The next day, he swept me off to Peru where I managed to twist my ankle on the way to see Machu Picchu. I did post some great pictures of the donkey that hauled me down if that's any consolation.

"Here," Beau says, thrusting a bottle of water into my hands the moment I walk off stage for my first wardrobe change. My wardrobe is a lot more complicated now. Gone are all of the skin-tight jumpsuits and crop tops. Now, I'm in roomier outfits. Yep, you guessed it. Six months into our marriage, I got pregnant.

It was planned. No failed birth control, super sperm, or any of that other stuff for me. We just decided we didn't want to wait to start a family.

Beau was beyond excited when that little stick showed two lines. It caused a few disagreements over me immediately beginning the tour. I worked out a compromise with the label to divide it into two sections with a six-month break in the middle.

"How are you feeling?" Robin asks when I reach the dressing room. I have two mother hens watching over me now.

"I'm good."

"I'll be glad when tonight is over," Beau says. His hand presses to my belly as I'm trying to wrestle my shirt off.

"As much as I hate to admit it, I will be too." Robin holds up my next outfit. "The barfing on the bus was bad enough. Now, I keep waiting for that thing to pop out during a performance."

"Nothing's popping out," I say, rolling my eyes. "I've still got three months. I'm not that huge, am I?"

"You're perfect," Beau answers. He's not an idiot either.

"Yeah, now get your perfect butt back out there." Robin helps me pull my next outfit into place. Quickly, we move back toward the stage. I notice out of the corner of my eye Beau taking his place on the side again. Arms still crossed over his chest, scowl still firmly in place.

I slip him a quick smile before turning to Luke. He's already begun the next song. It's going to be nice knowing I can take time away and still come back to the same guys I started with. They're actually excited about having extra time too.

Our songs are a little different with this album. I'm told they're softer. Less about tribulations and more about falling in love.

"Thank you for coming out tonight. I hope you had as much fun as we did," I say at the end of the last song. I announce the band one more time, and we're officially done for a while. We only return for one encore, then my feet need a break.

I thought first-time pregnancies weren't this hard on your body. Someone should explain that to this one. My feet and back are screaming.

"Sit," Beau barks when we reach the dressing room. "Robin, can you give us a couple of minutes." He's used to the fans traipsing through for the meet and greet by now. Robin nods and closes the door.

I sink onto the couch in relief. "Let me see these." Beau pulls my feet onto his lap. Carefully, he pulls off my boots. His thumbs rub circles across the arches.

"If I wasn't so tired, I'd ride you like there's no tomorrow just for doing that," I moan. He really does have magical hands.

"I think that's how we got here in the first place." He smirks at me. I know exactly how we got here. It involved the couch in his studio and a very risqué drawing session. Think Rose in *Titanic.* "Do you want to change?"

"No. Let's just get this done so we can go back to the hotel, and I can collapse." He slides my favorite slippers on and helps me off the couch. "How come I never realized until now that cozy slippers really are God's gift to the world?" He laughs and moves to the door. With his hand resting on the knob, he turns to appraise me.

"Hmm, I might have to disagree with that."

He opens the door, and Travis makes his entrance.

"Uncle Travis is here!" I swear I can hear Beau sigh from all the way across the room.

"Hey, don't forget Uncle Trace is here also." His bright eyes sweep over me the moment he enters the room. "How are you, sweetheart?" Great, now I have four mother hens all clucking around me.

"I'm great. Ready for some quiet time at home."

"Are you kidding?" Travis says. "We've got way too much to do. Bro softball league, get the nursery ready, graduation,"—he counts each one off on his fingers—"moving, baby classes, baby."

It all sounds exhausting, except for bro softball league. That's literally what they call it, and I can't believe they convinced Beau to play.

I can't wait to see our friends again. Austen started a book club last time I was home. It was probably all the wine I drank at one of the meetings that led to the naked sketching and this little one. Anyway, they always made sure I could join via online chat when I was on the road.

"All right," I say finally. "Let's get this done, so we can get onto that."

* * *

BEAU

I had no idea the difference one Christmas could make in my life. If you had told me I'd be balanced on a stool in the corner of a room watching my wife sign autographs, I would have laughed. Not only am I in awe that I have a wife, but I'm about to be a father. Now I'll get the chance to do everything right that I got wrong with Travis.

"Babe, are you ready to go?"

Babe. I'm someone's babe now.

"Whenever you are."

Robin ushers the last fan out the door. Harmony turns to me. She looks exhausted but gorgeous all at the same time. I take her hand, leaving Robin to pack up her stuff, and pull her to the door.

"I'm starving," she admits halfway down the hall.

"What are you starving for tonight?" I have hunted down the oddest food over the last six months when I'm with her. I actually stood outside the bakery one night in our small town, begging Lucy to sell me anything she had left. Harmony devoured a stale cinnamon roll and a blueberry bagel at two in the morning. Good thing Lucy, the owner, is so good-natured. I owe her big for that one.

"I want the biggest plate of enchiladas ever seen."

"They're going to give you indigestion," I warn.

"Beau, everything has started giving me indigestion. I swear the doctor is off by a couple of months."

"Let's hope not. I don't really want to deliver our kid on the way home tomorrow. Especially after enchiladas."

We have no idea if we're having a boy or a girl. I convinced Harmony to wait until it makes an appearance. Seemed like a fun surprise at the time. I think the whole town wants to kill me though. They're planning a huge baby shower with no idea what the theme should be.

There's a car waiting outside to whisk us to the hotel. It's one of the better perks of being the star of the show. We're staying at an upscale hotel not far from the venue.

Harmony, who looks dead on her feet, plasters on her best smile until we're locked safely in the room. She would never take a chance on disappointing a fan who happened to be in view.

"You head for the shower, and I'll order. Once again, are

you sure about the Mexican food at"—I check my watch—
"eleven at night?"

"Absolutely." She kicks off her slippers and walks to the bathroom shedding clothes along the way. "Chips and queso too," she calls from the bathroom.

All I can do is shake my head as I hear the water turn on. Finding Mexican food at eleven at night is no easy task. Even in the city on a Saturday night, most places are closed. Thankfully, Trace has a place on speed dial.

"Fuzzy robes might also be God's best gift to the world," she says, walking into the living area of our suite fifteen minutes later.

"Still beg to differ." She walks to me, and I envelop her in my arms. "Your night of indigestion should be here soon."

"My hero."

"I think that sentiment will change sometime in the middle of the night."

"Never." She gives me a radiant smile, and my heart rate increases threefold. I wonder if it will ever stop doing that. I don't think so. I don't think I will ever fall out of love with Harmony. There's a very good chance that my heart hammering in my chest will eventually kill me when I'm old just from one look. That's the plan anyway.

"Yay!" she exclaims when the desk calls. I meet the driver at the door and tip him well. Harmony is already bouncing in one of the chairs next to the table. "You're not eating anything?" She gazes at the carryout containers in front of her.

"There's only room for one of us in the bathroom all night." She shrugs and digs into the massive mess of food. With a deep sigh, she closes her eyes, and I watch as she celebrates the first bite.

"I hope you're as excited to go home as you are about your dinner," I tease.

She looks at me with her soft blue eyes. Her smile is radiant.

"I'm already home, Beau. You're here. You're the only home I'll ever need."

A warmth I'd never felt before her sweeps through my body. She's right. Over the last year, I've been home at the ranch and in Nashville. We've made our home on the back of a bus, in hotel rooms, dressing rooms, and stages.

I understand what she means. She's been my home since that first morning when she wrapped her arms around me in the middle of a snowstorm. I'll never need anything else. I'm home.

* * *

Thank you for reading Harmony for Christmas. I hope you enjoyed Beau and Harmony's story. Want more of the Dansboro Crossing series? Start at the beginning with, *Overdue*, here: https://books2read.com/u/4D8v6P

Don't miss another release. Sign up for my newsletter here: https://www.averysamson.com/contact

Justifiable

Inevitable

<u>The Sköll Ranch Shifter Series</u>

Sten

Dane

Arne

acknowledgments

Every year starting usually the day after Thanksgiving, I begin my epic reading journey of nothing but holiday romances. When I first decided to try my hand at writing my own, I settled on the idea of being snowed in with a cowboy/rancher. I'm not positive the times I've been snowed in at the ranch were ever this fun. Got a lot of reading done though.

Thanks to everyone who read, ARC read, shared, and reveiwed Beau and Harmony's story. I hope you noticed the mention of the budding Nashville star in Owen and Eliot's story.

As always, My Brother's Editor has turned my messy draft into something readable with commas in all the right places. And yes, a dirt tank is a real thing. I spent one snowed in weekend sliding down ours with a brother, just like Beau.

Where would I be without the talents of Literally Yours making sure I spread the word about each release. Ava is the best. Working with me when I throw out a surprise Christmas book can't be easy.

A special thank you to my forever patient partner in crime, Rachel McCarthy. Somehow, I've gone from nagging her to clean her room to getting me my cover. At least we're consistant. Love you!

Finally, thank you to the rest of my family. I could never

do this without their support. That includes the brother that announced loudly in the middle of the Dallas Country Club that I write porn. Keeping it classy. He did still tell me he was crazy proud of me. I'll take it.

about the author

Avery Samson grew up on a ranch outside of a small west Texas town. Since she could remember, she's had her face stuck in a book. High School graduation found her leaving ranch life for the big city.

After living all over the state of Texas, she now finds herself back on one of the family ranches near Dallas with her husband surrounded by cattle. A lot of them. They're every-where! When not traveling or reading, she spends her time writing.

Avery would love for you to follow her. She's everywhere (just like those damn cows.)

Join my newsletter for all the latest news.
averysamsonbooks.com/newsletter

Visit my website for my current book list.
averysamsonbooks.com

Join my reader group.
https://www.facebook.com/groups/216191437248096

Like me on Facebook.
https://www.facebook.com/averysamsonauthor

Follow me on Instagram.
https://www.instagram.com/averysamson91/

Watch my videos on TikTok.
https://www.tiktok.com/@averysamson91

Check out my Pinterest page.
https://www.pinterest.com/averysamson91/

www.ingramcontent.com/pod-product-compliance
Lightning Source LLC
Chambersburg PA
CBHW031557310726
48974CB00003B/705